Hansjörg Schneider, born in Aarau, Switzerland, in 1938, has worked as a teacher and journalist, and is one of the most performed playwrights in the German language. He is best known for his Inspector Hunkeler crime novels. *Hunkeler's Secret*, following on from the success of *The Murder of Anton Livius, Silver Pebbles* and *The Basel Killings*, is the fourth in the series to appear in English. Schneider has received numerous awards, among them the prestigious Friedrich Glauser Prize for *The Basel Killings*. He lives and writes in Basel.

# HUNKELER'S SECRET

Hansjörg Schneider

Translated by Astrid Freuler

**BITTER LEMON PRESS**
**LONDON**

BITTER LEMON PRESS

First published in the United Kingdom in 2025 by
Bitter Lemon Press, 47 Wilmington Square, London WC1X OET

www.bitterlemonpress.com

First published in German as HUNKELERS GEHEIMNIS
by Diogenes Verlag AG, Zurich, 2015

The translation of this work was supported by the Swiss Arts Council Pro Helvetia

The letter on page 183 from the head of the Basel cantonal
immigration authorities to councillor Fritz Brechbühl, dated
15 March 1939, was sourced from the following book:
Lukrezia Seiler and Jean-Claude Wacker, *Fast täglich kamen Flüchtlinge* (Refugees
arrived almost every day), Christoph Merian Verlag, Basel, 2013.

A CIP record for this book is available from the British Library

PB ISBN 978–1–916725-126
eB USC ISBN 978–1–916725-133
eB ROW ISBN 978–1–916725-140

Typeset by Tetragon, London
Printed and bound by CPI Group (UK) Ltd, Croydon CRO 4YY

swiss arts council
prohelvetia

Peter Hunkeler, former inspector with the Basel City criminal investigation department, now retired, woke up and didn't know where he was.

As he opened his eyes, he saw broad daylight. Above him was a white ceiling, and dangling down from it was something like a hand grip with a cord. The air smelled odd. Not like it did in his old farmhouse in Alsace, where it always smelled of grass and damp earth. And not like in his Basel apartment, which smelled of him, Hunkeler. The air here seemed clinically clean.

He felt calm, relaxed and pain-free. He noticed he was lying on his back. Odd, he usually slept on his side, in the foetal position. He looked up again, at the hand grip. Where had that come from all of a sudden? Who had put it there? It wasn't hanging from the ceiling, as he'd first thought, but from a metal arm that reached across the bed. And the cord was actually a call bell.

Now Hunkeler remembered where he was. In a hospital, more specifically in a hospital bed. He'd been operated on early this morning.

He carefully ran his hands over his chest and belly. Down between his legs was something that didn't belong there. And now it was all coming back to him. He'd been admitted to Basel's Merian Iselin Hospital yesterday, 7 March, in the early evening. First thing this morning, he'd been given an injection that had sent him into a deep sleep. He had requested this, as he didn't want to be aware of the preparations for the surgery.

At nine, he'd come round again. His girlfriend Hedwig had been there, holding his hand. Everything is OK, she had whispered. A nurse had explained that the procedure had taken just under half an hour. No carcinoma, everything was fine. Presumably, they had then transferred him to this room. He hadn't been aware of it, he'd instantly fallen back asleep again after the good news.

"You have a catheter," he heard a man say. "It's not too bad, you get used to it. And as you're drugged up, you should be feeling pleasantly pain-free. Am I right?"

"I'm not sure," Hunkeler replied and was alarmed at his own voice. It sounded feeble and hoarse. "They've sliced open my belly and you're telling me I should be feeling fine? Do you know what I would normally do with a guy who does that kind of thing to me?"

"I'm assuming by 'guy' you mean Dr Fahedin," the voice came back. "He's an internationally renowned expert. You should be grateful that it was him who operated on you and not just any old klutz."

"I would punch him in the face. The cheek of it! Assaulting me like that while I'm asleep. A person's dignity and integrity are sacrosanct. That's what it says in the Human Rights Act. Does that no longer apply in hospitals?"

He could feel a distant pain in his belly; it seemed to be coming closer.

"Go ahead, shout. Or at least try to. It'll draw you back to life. And by the way, he didn't slice your belly open. He operated through the urethra. You're a lucky devil."

Hunkeler looked to his left, where the voice was coming from. He saw a man with a bald head and sunken cheeks sitting in the bed next to his.

"How would you know? Who are you, anyway?"

"Dr Stephan Fankhauser, pleased to meet you. And you are Inspector Peter Hunkeler. I enquired with the nurse. She told me about your operation. I must congratulate you."

"You're getting on my nerves," said Hunkeler. "Can't you keep quiet?"

"I'm afraid that's not possible. I can't keep quiet, I have to talk. Otherwise I'll perish. Talking is the only form of living I have left. Only words help to stem the tide of time."

The man laughed hoarsely.

"These are the sentences I still need to say. They sound good, don't you think? Even though I'm talking nonsense. Do you understand?"

"No."

"But you're a well-educated man. You went to university."

"How do you know?"

The man pointed to a laptop lying on the bed beside him.

"It's all in here. You seem to be an interesting person. We should have a chat."

"I'm not interesting. I'm a poor old sod. Can't you see that?"

"You're in shock after the operation, that's all. Close your eyes, relax."

Hunkeler closed his eyes and tried to slow his breath. Stephan Fankhauser. The name sounded familiar. "Red Steff," he said. "I remember you from 1968. One of the biggest troublemakers of the student movement. You had hair down to your shoulders back then."

"That's right. And then what?"

"Then you joined a left-leaning law firm. Later, you became the director of the Basel Volksbank. Bourgeois through and through. And strait-laced. You should be ashamed of yourself."

"That's it. Go ahead and insult me if it makes you feel better."

"It doesn't make me feel better," Hunkeler barked, and got a fright when the distant pain made itself felt again. He decided not to attempt any more shouting.

"And what about you, Inspector? Weren't you a member of Basel's leftist student group, LIST? How does that square with going on to join the CID? Back in the day, we viewed the likes of you as the henchmen of the capitalist bourgeoisie. Wasn't that a moral conflict you struggled with?"

"Not really. I wasn't a member of LIST, just a sympathizer."

"So a liberal jerk who didn't want to get his hands dirty."

"Rubbish. Anyway, I didn't turn into a henchman of capitalism, I was simply a man who had to earn a living. I had a family. I carried out my work as best I could."

"And drawing a nice pension now, of course."

Hunkeler was thinking hard. It was good, it took his mind away from this damned hospital bed. "And you?" he asked Fankhauser. "Weren't you given the boot? For accepting large amounts of untaxed money from abroad?"

"Not at all. In our circles people aren't given the boot. They are thanked for their excellent service and pensioned off with a golden handshake."

"That's not what I've heard."

"Because you keep bad company. Indeed, one should only move in the very best circles. By which I mean rich circles. Because the world never changes, not even through revolutions. It took me a long time to realize that. Once I had, I acted accordingly."

"I heard you received a pay-off to the tune of several million. Hush money. Enough to afford any luxury you want for the rest of your life."

"If only I could still live a life. As you can see, that's not possible."

"True. Our argument is purely hypothetical. I hereby end it."

Hunkeler closed his eyes again, but Fankhauser was persistent.

"Please don't end our conversation. At least listen to me."

"Why didn't you take a private room? You could certainly afford it."

"I did have a private room. I nearly died of loneliness. You, Inspector Hunkeler, are a gift from heaven."

Hunkeler covered his ears. It was no good; Fankhauser's voice was too sonorous.

"I've had four abdominal operations. A fifth one isn't possible. Consequently, the cancer continues to grow. Very rapidly, by the way. And I have diabetes too. I get insulin injected twice a day. I'm basically waiting for death."

"We're all doing that."

"It depends on how you're waiting though. From a philosophical viewpoint, living is nothing more than preparing for death, as Montaigne said."

"Not true. Montaigne said philosophizing is preparing for death, not living."

"Wonderful, brilliant," Fankhauser replied. "I knew you'd be good to argue with. We all carry death in us. You too, Inspector. Perhaps you'll even die before me."

"You'd be happy about that, would you?"

"No, on the contrary. I don't have anyone, apart from my son. He visited me once. Then he rang and told me he wouldn't be coming again. He said he can't bear hospitals."

"I can understand that. I can't bear them either."

"Just do what I do. I'm high on morphine."

"Then I suggest you float off and stop waffling on!" Hunkeler barked.

That night, Hunkeler lay awake. A white, shimmering light hovered above him, reflected by the ceiling. It looked serene, almost magical. Evidently it was snowing outside.

It all seemed rather surreal. He felt oddly removed into a pain-free timelessness that put him in an almost cheerful mood. He heard the bell in a nearby church tower strike midnight, twelve hard, precise tolls. He heard Fankhauser muttering to himself.

"Why am I not in pain?" Hunkeler asked.

"You're still alive, thank goodness," Fankhauser replied. "You're listening to me."

"I'm not listening. I'm wondering what on earth I'm doing here."

He propped himself up to look across at his neighbour, who was lying in bed semi-reclined.

"Don't you ever sleep?"

"No. I go round in circles, all day and all night. The circles keep getting tighter. There's no way out, it's a spiral. In the end I will arrive in the centre. I will arrive in myself. That's when I'll die. But for now I'm still spinning round. And I want you to help me go round by listening to me."

"No," barked Hunkeler, and it already sounded more like shouting. "Spare me. I can't be doing with all this spinning."

Fankhauser turned his head towards Hunkeler, a bare, emaciated skull, almost lipless. He raised his right hand, it looked like the hand of a skeleton. "Please, we were at university together," he pleaded. "We fought together, for a better world."

"Hardly. I'm not the fighting type."

"Oh yes you are. You come from a humble background, like me."

"What makes you think that?"

"I can tell. We both carved out a career for ourselves."

"Please don't talk about me. My life is my business."

"Why the shame?"

"I'm not ashamed. I joined the CID because I like working with people."

"We really went for it back then, you, me, everyone involved in LIST. We gave the high and mighty of this city a proper scare. Can you remember all the daughters and sons of Basel's richest and most distinguished families that joined us? That frightened those in power. They couldn't exactly have the police beat up the rich kids. And do you remember the meetings we held on that estate? It belonged to a family who owned one of the big pharmaceutical companies. There we were, with Vietcong badges on our collars and the words of Chairman Mao in our pockets, and the lady of the manor brought us wine from her cellar. Do you remember that?"

Yes, Hunkeler remembered. But he didn't reply.

"It's amazing how many of us went on to climb the career ladder," Fankhauser continued. "Parliamentarians, chief editors, directors in industry and finance. Not in the military though, but that's falling apart anyway."

Fankhauser's chuckle quickly turned into a rasping cough, which he tried to suppress, probably because coughing would take too much strength.

"Look at me. I talked about the global revolution. How everything needed to change, especially the distribution of goods. I waffled on about class consciousness, about the permanent revolution, about the need to use force, to take up arms and fight. But look at Fidel Castro. He was our idol, and of course he really had taken up arms. What became of him? A run-of-the-mill dictator. And the only reason Che Guevara remained popular is because he died young. I wonder what would have become of Jesus of Nazareth if he'd grown old. Perhaps a banker with the Vatican Bank, the bank of the Holy Spirit. Eventually they all end up chasing the money, the idealists. Because money is the only form of power that counts. When I finally grasped that, I went to work for a bank. I didn't want to work on the edge of society, I wanted to be at the centre of power. Do you understand that, Inspector?"

"Yes, but I think you should focus on saving your soul."

"That's exactly what I'm trying to do. I'm trying to explain to myself how I came to be where I am, lying in this bed next to yours, glad to have found a listener."

"Well," said Hunkeler, "I've definitely had enough. You'll have to excuse me." He reached for the bell button and pushed it.

"That's a pity," said Fankhauser. "If you can't bear listening to me any longer, I'll just whisper from now on. But it's rather sad when you're told to die wordlessly."

The door opened. A petite woman in a white coat appeared. She was wearing a blue headscarf.

"I need a sleeping pill please," said Hunkeler. "I can't cope with my neighbour any more. He keeps going on and on, talking pseudo-philosophical nonsense."

The woman nodded. Her eyes seemed to be smiling. Were they dark brown? He couldn't quite see. Wordlessly, she took a pill from her coat pocket and gave it to him. He noticed her hand was beautifully shaped, with a small diamond ring on the middle finger. Hunkeler took the pill and washed it down with the glass of water she handed him. She nodded, smiled again and left.

"Good night then," said Hunkeler.

The following day, Hedwig came around noon. She brought him the apples, bananas and newspapers he'd asked for.

"This hospital slop is inedible," he claimed. "It tastes of nothing."

"Did you try it at least?"

He shook his head in disgust. "No. One has to retain some level of autonomy in this madhouse. It's no good caving in completely."

She smiled at him. "Go on, have a rant, it'll do you good. And by the way, they're happy with how you're doing." She looked around the room. Her gaze fell on Fankhauser, who was lying propped up in bed as always.

Hunkeler saw the alarm on her face. "That's Dr Fankhauser," he told her. "Formerly known as Red Steff, revolutionary leader of Basel's leftist student group, most recently boss of the Volksbank. He's being quiet for once. He usually jabbers on incessantly."

"Pleased to meet you, Madame," said Fankhauser. "We rarely have lady visitors here." He lifted his arm to shake her hand.

Hedwig backed away, startled.

"I'm sorry, Madame. I know my appearance is not particularly pleasant these days. I'll leave you in peace."

"What a gentleman," Hunkeler commented. "I know him from university. He's in a pretty bad way."

There was a violent coughing by way of reply, followed by a wheezy grunt.

"I'm supposed to go for a walk with you," said Hedwig.

"What? Are you mad? I can barely stand."

"The nurse told me to, so come on." She pulled him up.

He looked out the window, it was snowing heavily out there. "I'm not going outside with that snowstorm going on," he insisted.

"Nobody expects you to. We're going to take the stairs up to the cafeteria. Come on, get dressed."

Out in the hallway she hugged him tight. Her arms were trembling.

"What's the matter with you?" he asked. "Who's the patient here, me or you?"

"It gave me a fright, Peter. That man looks like a living skeleton. He even wanted to shake my hand."

He stroked her hair. "It's not all that bad. I think he's quite glad to be dying. But us two, we'll manage to struggle on for a while yet, won't we? Now let's go, I need a coffee."

Up in the cafeteria they sat down by a window facing west. The snow had stopped falling and the sun was breaking through the clouds. A surreal light set everything aglow, the roofs of the city, the nearest hill across the border in Alsace, the white water tower of Folgensbourg.

"Beautiful," said Hunkeler. "Actually, I'm feeling fine again already. We could drive straight over to our house this evening, light the fire and drink a bottle of wine."

"You're staying here for as long as the doctors tell you to," she replied.

"I can't stand much more of the guy in the other bed. He's spewing out his entire past, right in front of my feet. Even though I'm not the slightest bit interested. But he's merciless."

She lowered her gaze and went quiet.

"What's up?" he asked.

"Your daughter Isabelle has asked me to pass on her regards."

He was taken aback. He hadn't been expecting that.

"She says she hopes you get well soon."

Isabelle, whom he hadn't seen for years. Who had distanced herself from him early on and had completely cut ties at eighteen.

"Aren't you pleased?"

"I am. But I don't want to talk about it. Or rather, I can't."

The last he'd heard from her was that she had given birth to a daughter called Estelle and had moved to a village in the Vosges mountains.

"You mean you don't want to."

"Perhaps. I don't like thinking back to that time."

"That's a pity."

"Why?"

"Because it interests me."

"Isabelle was my open wound for a long time. It only healed when I met you. Really, it's true. You helped me get over it."

He reached to take her hand, but suddenly grew suspicious.

"Anyway, what exactly is going on? I mean, how did you find her?"

"I rang her and told her that you were having an operation."

"What? Behind my back?"

"Well of course. What do you think? You can't bury your past, it won't work."

He stared at her in disbelief. But he stood no chance against her resolve.

"So, are you saying you regularly speak to her? And since when?"

"Ever since you told me about her."

"And all in secret, without a single word?"

"Of course. Someone has to be sensible here."

Towards evening, Hunkeler got a visit from Madörin, former detective sergeant, now Hunkeler's successor as inspector. They hadn't seen much of each other since Hunkeler had retired. He'd been avoiding Madörin. He simply didn't like the guy. His squat, stocky figure, his hangdog look. He knew Madörin was a capable criminal investigator. But Hunkeler had always felt that being a good inspector required more than just tenacious implacability, it required kindness and compassion towards people.

Now Madörin was standing next to Hunkeler's hospital bed with a bunch of flowers in his hand. He clearly felt embarrassed, seeing his former boss lying there in his nightshirt. "I'm bringing you these flowers on behalf of the CID," he announced. "With best wishes for a speedy recovery."

"Thank you."

"In particular Corporal Lüdi and Haller send their regards."

Madörin looked around the room for somewhere to put the flowers.

"Lay them on the table," Hunkeler instructed. "Personally, I think flowers in a hospital are intolerable. They remind me of funerals."

Madörin did as he was told, indignantly shaking his head. He didn't like being bossed around.

"And Prosecutor Suter?" Hunkeler asked.

"He sends his regards too. I spoke to him on the phone. He's currently at a conference in Cologne. And warm wishes from Frau Held at reception."

"Thank you."

It was all Hunkeler could say, even though he would have liked to be a little more friendly. He felt touched, thinking of the many years they'd spent together, the power battles they'd fought, most of which he'd won, the successful investigations and the failed ones.

"Nice room you've got here," said Madörin. "Quite luxurious." He looked around, distrustful and aloof. He was always on duty. "Who's that?" he asked, glancing across to the other bed.

"Dr Fankhauser, former director of the Basel Volksbank," Hunkeler told him. "I'm sure you've heard of him."

Madörin furrowed his brow, as always when he was thinking hard. "Oh yes." And to Fankhauser, "How are you?"

"Commensurate with circumstances, thanks," Fankhauser replied. "I assume you're from the police?"

"Yes, CID. Actually, we've just received a report stating that Viktor Waldmeier has been arrested while entering the US. He's your successor at the Volksbank, isn't he?"

A gentle smile spread across Fankhauser's face, a hint of vitality. "Ah, Viktor. I knew he'd slip up on one of his deals one day. But what do they expect from us? Everyone wants to earn money from the banks. But when a deal backfires, we bankers have to take the fall. By the way, if you want to arrest me, go ahead, be my guest." He gave a wheezy laugh, which turned into an agonizing cough.

"Stop it," Hunkeler told Madörin. "Leave him in peace, he's in a really bad way." Then, very quietly, "Is that true about Waldmeier?"

"Yes, at Kennedy Airport in New York. But it's not official yet."

"Well I never."

"Yes, old pal, quite a lot has changed since you left. We're interlinked like crazy, in every direction, with every possible service. Good clean police work has gone out of fashion. Just be glad you're not involved any more."

Was he gloating now, or did he mean it?

"I really mean that, by the way. Honest. Sometimes I miss you."

*

Hunkeler had eaten two bananas and an apple. The bananas had tasted great, unlike the apple. It was one of those new varieties and looked like it was straight out of the Garden of Eden: red-cheeked, yellow-speckled and bursting with juice. But biting into one of these overbred beauties was like walking into a hair salon. It tasted of perfume. And cheap perfume at that. No character, no acidity, nothing. As interchangeable as the numbskulls that ate these things. And now he, Hunkeler, was one of them.

He grinned bitterly at the thought. He felt ancient. Like a fossil from the third day of creation, when the Almighty had separated land from sea; a relic that had surfaced and landed right here in this hospital bed. He looked across at his neighbour, who was lying with his knees bent up and muttering incomprehensibly. So that's what progress looked like when the end was near. Lying in a bed, in an unfamiliar room. Being cared for by strangers whose names you don't know. Like that petite young woman, of whom Hunkeler couldn't even have said what colour her eyes were. And you're grateful if an old inspector is in the next bed, someone you can exchange a few words with. Then, when you're finally dead, you're shunted out of the room and into the elevator that takes you down to the morgue. Hours later or perhaps two or three days later, depending on how many corpses are accruing, you're incinerated somewhere or other. And not a word about it, done and dusted.

Hunkeler felt out of place. Like a vegetable, a carrot that due to a silly system fault has ended up in the compartment for frozen meat, wrapped in plastic, neatly vacuum-packed. He would have liked to remove the catheter and quietly abscond. But was that even possible? Wasn't the reception desk staffed around the clock, to intercept fleeing patients?

He thought about Madörin claiming that he missed Hunkeler. Was he really being missed? Wasn't it the other way round? That Hunkeler was longing for Madörin, even though the man annoyed him? Perhaps that's what Hunkeler was hankering after. The power battles, the daily arguments.

He turned his head to the bedside table and looked at the alarm clock. Half past twelve, middle of the night. He listened, wondering if he could pick up any other sounds apart from the constant mumbling from the other bed. Footsteps, voices, a shout. Nothing – the entire hospital seemed to be asleep.

"The time one has lived continually increases," said Hunkeler. "And the time one still has to live perpetually diminishes. That's a platitude, but it's the sad truth."

"Thank goodness," Fankhauser said. "You're still here. You're listening to me."

"I'm not. I'm just saying that this erosion starts way back in childhood. But you're not aware of it yet, because you're happy to be getting older. It's a different matter once you're old. You brace yourself against the passing of time, even though that's ridiculous, because time passes anyway."

"I've heard you have a daughter."

Hunkeler hesitated, wondering whether to answer or not. "Yes, sort of."

"And? Were you a good father?"

"No. Our paths separated quite early on."

"You see? The only thing that was important, you failed at. I'm currently enumerating all my failings. I have a whole list of them. I keep reciting them to myself to make sure I'm still alive. The list grows longer every time. I'm wallowing in my faults. Perhaps human life is nothing but a big mistake, who knows?"

"Nonsense. You should be ashamed of yourself," said Hunkeler.

"Why?"

"Because there is no true life within a false life, as Theodor Adorno said. Have you forgotten that? Besides, we all rejected the nuclear family because we saw it as a capitalist tool for domestication."

"And yet you got married?" Fankhauser wondered.

"Yes. We wanted to give it a go. Also, my girlfriend was pregnant. It was expected of us that we marry."

"And where is your former girlfriend now?"

"She died a few years ago."

"And your daughter?"

"She lives in the Vosges mountains, as far as I know."

"So you alienated yourself from your own daughter."

"Nonsense. I let her get on with her life. I hope she's happy."

From outside, a church clock could be heard striking.

"Do you really never sleep?"

"No," said Fankhauser. "I need to do my calculations. In the end, when I die, I have to know the score. Debit and credit. Do you understand? There's a lot listed under debit, almost nothing under credit."

"Despite your millions?"

"Oh come on, money is muck. The more you have of it, the dirtier it makes you."

"That's not true. Only those who don't have any money have to get their hands dirty when they work. You don't. And

I'm sure you don't live in the narrow streets of Kleinbasel, among the Turks and Albanians. You probably live up in the clean air of the Bruderholz district."

"Yes, except that now I live here in this hospital room, lonely and forsaken. Apart from you, of course. And I'm very grateful to you for that."

"You're welcome. But I'm afraid that's it for now. I need to get some sleep." Hunkeler reached for the bell button and pushed it.

"Do you know who I'm bequeathing my money to?" Fankhauser asked. "Are you curious?"

"Your son, I assume."

More coughing from Fankhauser, followed by a terrible rasping wheeze.

"Wrong. He's only getting the compulsory share. I've bequeathed everything else to Basel Zoo. My son will be surprised when he hears that. He will curse me. But that's what I'm like. Society has made me what I am. A monster. This, it would seem, was my destiny in late capitalism. Zero solidarity, zero comradeship. *Homo homini lupus.* Man is a wolf to another man. A rapacious, fierce animal that attacks members of its own species. Do you understand what I'm saying, Inspector? Say something, answer me. Do you think I'm a monster too?"

"I think it serves Viktor Waldmeier right," Hunkeler replied. "It's about time some of your kind are convicted and locked up."

Again the terrible rasping wheeze, the gasping for air.

"Wrong, you're totally wrong. You're still fantasizing, Inspector. Waldmeier will never be convicted. He knows too much. He's not stupid, he has something up his sleeve.

He will sell his inside knowledge, the bank data he's bound to have with him. He's going to sell it to the Americans for millions of dollars and betray the Volksbank without batting an eye. Then he'll retire and lead a jolly life somewhere by a pleasant beach."

This was simply too much for Hunkeler. "Who's in charge in Switzerland?" he shouted. "Us or the Americans?"

"See, I knew it," said Fankhauser. "You're ranting like a proper Swiss. Good, very good. But completely ineffective, because the stronger side rules. And the weaker side has to obey. The Americans are stronger. It's as simple as that."

"We have direct democracy in Switzerland," Hunkeler objected. "In a direct democracy, the people rule. It's the people who decide which rules apply in Switzerland and which don't."

Hunkeler was a little surprised at the words that were spilling out of him. But he was speaking from the bottom of his heart. When all was said and done, he firmly believed in the Swiss democratic system.

"A proper old-school Swiss confederate," Fankhauser observed. "Glad to hear it. But you know yourself that it's pure folklore."

"No," Hunkeler disagreed. "Switzerland is a free, sovereign nation. That's a fact."

Fankhauser seemed to delight in the heated discussion. He chuckled wheezily. "A Swiss confederation in which everyone stands side by side, collectively discussing and deciding what should be done. How lovely," he remarked. "But this federation has long gone, it only exists in our dreams and imagination. Perhaps it still works on a local level, when the good citizens go and vote on the increase in dog tax and suchlike. Fair enough. But the important decisions that affect Switzerland are no longer made in this federation, they haven't been for a long time. Even our banks, which count among the most powerful financial institutions in the world, are no longer free to make their own decisions. It's the Americans who dictate the rules for the Swiss banks. Nobody gives a damn whether that's fair or not."

Hunkeler didn't respond. He felt too tired and washed out.

"Years ago," Fankhauser continued, "if you wanted to make a lot of money, you had to set up your own bank. That's no longer necessary. Now you just have to work in a bank. Then you can steal confidential data and sell it abroad for lots of money. And that's exactly what Viktor Waldmeier is going to do."

"Enough talk. I want to sleep now."

"OK, I'll leave you in peace. But I'd like to thank you for the stimulating discussion."



A little later, the door finally opened and a petite woman in a white coat appeared. She was wearing a blue headscarf, like the previous night.

"I need a sleeping pill," Hunkeler told her. "A strong one, please. What's your name, if I may ask?"

She placed her index finger on her lips. A faint scent of cinnamon surrounded her. It was barely detectable, but distinct.

"It doesn't disturb Mr Fankhauser if we talk," he said. "We had quite an animated conversation earlier. He's probably exhausted now."

Her eyes seemed to be smiling. Were they greenish-grey? Her face was delicate, like porcelain. She gave him the pill and he washed it down with a gulp of water. He saw that she was wearing a ruby on her right middle finger. She was still smiling and gave him a friendly nod.

"Good night then," he said.

She remained standing beside his bed. The cinnamon scent was very noticeable now. He wanted to say something about it, pay her a compliment about how good she smelled. He decided to leave it. He could feel the pill starting to work.

After a while, when he was already drifting off to sleep, he saw her take a syringe out of her coat pocket and walk over to Fankhauser's bed. She folded back his blanket and exposed his belly. "What are you doing, nurse?" Fankhauser asked. "I don't need an injection now. Not until the morning." He raised his hands to defend himself, but he was too weak. With a quick, decisive movement, she rammed the syringe into his belly.

It was the strange ruthlessness that alarmed Hunkeler. Who was this woman who suddenly and mercilessly stabbed a patient like that? Was he dreaming? Was he trapped in a nightmare in which a young, beautiful woman appeared as an avenging angel? He tried to lift his right hand and say something, but he couldn't.

The woman pulled out the syringe. She remained standing by the bed, waiting motionlessly.

"You shouldn't have done that," said Fankhauser. "On no account." He tried to get up, summoning his last ounce of strength, but he sank back down onto the bed again. His breath became laboured and he began to pant. He gasped for air with his mouth torn open, several times. Then he grew limp. Silence. No breath, nothing.

The woman was still standing there, completely still, gazing at Fankhauser's face. After a while she put the syringe back into her pocket. She did this very slowly. It was as though she was waking from a dream. Then she turned away and looked over at Hunkeler, who still had his eyes open. A gentle smile appeared on her face. She nodded at him and placed her index finger on her lips. Then she left the room.

The following morning Hunkeler was so groggy from the pill he could barely open his eyes. When they brought him his breakfast, he saw that the other bed was empty. This didn't particularly worry him. After a few gulps of coffee he fell straight back to sleep.

At around ten, an assistant doctor told him Dr Fankhauser had passed away during the night. Hunkeler was instantly wide awake.

"So suddenly? What did he die of?"

"Heart failure," the doctor replied. "He had been terminally ill for some time."

"Perhaps, but he was still engaging in spirited debates with me."

"I know. It was his way of fighting against death. But he fell asleep peacefully in the end. When the night nurse did her last inspection round at half past five, all she could do was record his death. No doubt it's better for him that he could go."

"What's the name of this night nurse?"

"Lydia Siegenthaler. She's a medical student."

"Was she the same nurse as the previous night?"

"Yes, of course. She's on night duty all week. Why?"

"I had a terrible dream last night."

Hunkeler stayed in hospital for five days. On the morning of the sixth day he insisted on being discharged. They would have liked to keep him there another two nights, but he'd had enough.

At home, in his apartment on Mittlere Strasse, he mainly laid in bed dozing. Sometimes he tried to read, although that didn't work too well at first. He kept falling asleep, with the open book in his hand.

He'd bought himself two thick tomes about the First World War. Novels hadn't featured on his reading list for some time. Invented stories bored him, he was hungry for facts. He wanted to know why and how the big killing that caused Europe's downfall had started a hundred years ago.

He didn't want anyone to visit him, not even Hedwig. He needed to sink back into himself first, he told her. Eat apples, oranges and bananas, drink tea, and let things settle after the interference into his abdomen. The body isn't so quick to forget what has happened to it, he said.

Now, on this late morning of 17 March, he was sitting in his small car, driving along Hegenheimerstrasse towards the border. The rain was pouring down. The left wiper was scraping against the glass; he should have replaced it ages ago. In front of him was a heavy truck with a container full of building rubble. Its brake lights suddenly flared up. Hunkeler had to slam his foot on the brake pedal. He could feel his heart throbbing, it was beating fast. Take it steady, old man, he said to himself. You don't need to be anywhere, you've got all the time in the world.

The first allotments appeared, then the shaft tower of the gravel quarry, barely discernible in the rain-swept fog. Gravel mounds rose side by side, torn from the bedrock of the Rhine Valley, sorted according to size. Rusty diggers and cement mixers, some wrecked cars. Then the two small customs buildings, unoccupied and dark.

He felt himself relax. It was always like that when he drove across the border. The rain was still pelting down, making it hard to steer a steady course, but it seemed different somehow, calmer, steadier.

When he reached Hegenheim he pulled up outside the butcher's shop. He bought ham, liver pâté and sausages. Then he went into the bakery next door and got a baguette. It seemed as if nothing could happen to him now. He drove on feeling almost cheerful.

On the edge of Hésingue stood an old farmhouse with a large projecting roof. That was where his younger self had once waited for six hours, until someone stopped to give him a lift. He and his friend, both seventeen, had decided to hitchhike to Paris. They had stood here, patiently, full of confidence. The big wide world was waiting for them.

He remembered this every time he drove past here. And every time he was surprised that this waiting had embedded itself in his memory so clearly and beautifully.

Now an old man in a red jacket was standing there. He had a backpack and was holding out his thumb for a ride towards Altkirch. A hitchhiker. Hunkeler was surprised, but recognized him immediately. It was the artist Christian Moor, from Basel. He had owned an old half-timbered house in Knoeringue, but as far as Hunkeler had heard, he'd recently sold it.

Hunkeler stopped, leaned across and opened the passenger door.

"What on earth are you doing here? Come on, I'll give you a lift."

"Thank you."

Moor got in and pulled the door closed. He had three-day stubble and long, grey hair from which water was dripping down into his collar. There was a strong smell of wine. He fixed his eyes straight ahead.

Hunkeler switched off the engine. "What's going on?" he asked Moor.

"I absconded, early this morning," the painter replied. "I walked all the way here. Now I'm done in, I've got no strength left."

Hunkeler searched his jacket pocket for cigarettes and lit one. He immediately felt dizzy, so he threw it out the window.

"Where did you abscond from?"

"From Friedmatt hospital."

"And why were you at the Friedmatt?"

Moor now turned his head and looked at Hunkeler. His eyes were pale blue, bloodshot, and full of fear.

"What is this? An interrogation?"

"Yes," Hunkeler replied. "I can see you're not well."

"I set fire to my storeroom."

"With your paintings in it?"

"I wanted to destroy them all. I don't know why exactly. I just couldn't bear seeing my paintings any more. At first it was a bright, strong fire. Then it died down and smouldered away. I tried to put it out with the fire extinguisher. That's when I lost consciousness. My next-door neighbour, who has a carpenter's workshop, found me."

"Jesus!" said Hunkeler. "You've got yourself in a right mess there."

"I'm not going back to the Friedmatt. Absolutely not. All they want to do is to make sure you don't kill yourself. They're not interested in anything else. Keep you quiet, that's what they want to do. But what's life if not a continuous state of disquiet? Quiet is what we become in the grave."

Moor fished a plastic bag out of the rucksack.

"There's eight kinds of tablets in here. For falling asleep, for waking up, and to make you forget your problems during the day. The bosses at the pharmaceutical companies make millions with these, here in Basel too. I've had enough of that." He opened the passenger door and threw the bag out.

"Nobody can force you to stay at the Friedmatt," said Hunkeler. "Not unless you're at acute risk of committing suicide."

"Aren't we all? Perhaps we should all commit suicide. Then the whole sorry tale would finally come to an end. Don't you think?"

Hunkeler lit a second cigarette. He took three deep drags, it seemed to do him good now.

"Perhaps you should carry on taking the tablets, for a little while at least. The doctors know what they're doing."

"No, never again. Red wine is better." Moor tried to smile. It didn't work too well. "Why do you care, anyway? Why are you even listening to me?"

"Because I've got time."

"That's unusual. Nobody else seems to have time. Not in the Friedmatt either. Nobody wants to listen. Everyone wants to do the talking. That's the illness of our time, don't you think?"

"You're philosophizing," commented Hunkeler. "That's good. It means you're feeling better. Where do you want to go, anyway?"

"To Knoeringue, to the inn."

Hunkeler started the engine and pulled out onto the road again. They drove along the tree-lined avenue up to the high plain. At the top, the rain turned into flurries of snow. The fields stretched out white, absorbed by a soft mist that obscured everything.

"Paradise," said Moor. "A hundred years ago, artists used to travel to Morocco because they wanted to paint in the bright African light. But look at these hues of white and grey here. How they blend together and embrace each other. That's the real challenge for a painter, this symbiosis of white and grey."

"Hearing you talk like that, I know you're going to paint again," commented Hunkeler. And a little later: "What you did, that was arson. Even though it was your own belongings you set fire to. Strictly speaking, it's a matter for the police."

"Are you serious? I thought you were retired."

"True. Let's forget about it."

At Trois Maisons Hunkeler turned off left. Slush covered the road. Over by the forest edge, the outline of a concrete bunker could be made out. An elongated, stranded relic from the First or Second World War, or perhaps from prehistoric times. They passed a stream, a few crows on a harvested maize field. Then the first houses of Knoeringue appeared. Handsome half-timbered buildings with dark oak-wood beams and gleaming, pale infill. At the centre of the village stood the Gothic church, surrounded by the graveyard. Next to it was the Stollers' inn.

"Are you in good hands here?" Hunkeler asked.

"Yes. The landlady is a friend of mine. Thank you. You should come by sometime, share a bottle with me."

"I will."

Hunkeler carried on driving along the Hundsbach valley. It was a broad, open landscape. On a clear day you could see the Vosges mountains to the north-west. Now the only things visible were a stream, bushes, pastures and alder trees. Not a soul was about, the snow on the road lay untouched.

Moor's comment about the symbiosis of white and grey came to his mind, how they embraced each other. Wasn't that perhaps an articulation of depression? The man was afflicted, Hunkeler had realized that straight away. He wasn't drunk, despite the bloodshot eyes. Was it responsible to leave him alone with his troubles?

But Moor was right, Hunkeler was retired. The misery of strangers no longer concerned him. Other people were in charge of that now.

He remembered an exhibition of Moor's work he had visited decades ago, in a prestigious gallery. Purely formal, abstract pictures that had a peculiar affinity to real landscapes. White and grey. A grey that seemed to press in from the edges, into the white, gradually taking possession of it, absorbing it. They were beautiful, mysterious paintings. And Moor's work had sold well.

Hunkeler had always wondered about artists like Moor who painted the same picture all their lives, or rather tried to paint it. Evidently they never quite succeeded, otherwise they wouldn't keep on trying. Presumably it was all about the attempt, not the perfection.

Hunkeler parked in front of his house. The two cats, recognizing the sound of his engine, came running. The tabby in front and behind it the black and white one, which was more timid.

He went in and lit the fires, first in the kitchen stove, then in the living room, and put the kettle on. Next he went out to the henhouse to see if there were any eggs. He found two. He took them and watched the hens for a while as they scratched around in the snow. Fritz the cockerel was joining in too, even though he looked more like a half-plucked broiler chicken than a proud cockerel.

"Fritz, my old champ," Hunkeler said to him, "good to see you're holding up. You're retired, but you're still scratching about in the snow and pecking at the grass. Hang on in there, keep pecking. The snow will soon be gone. Spring will come and you'll be back to crowing at dawn like you did in your prime."

In the evening, Hedwig came. They sat in the warm kitchen, eating ham and liver pâté and the two eggs, and opened a bottle of Beaujolais.

Hedwig told him about her work at the kindergarten, which was in an ethnically diverse neighbourhood. "The kids are no problem at all," she said. "They're used to the fact that not everyone speaks the same language. I get on pretty well with the mothers too. They're a bit mistrustful at first, but once they get to know me they let me get on with it. But some of the fathers are obnoxious. Today I had a guy shouting at me because he didn't want his daughter to learn Basel dialect. But in this city, we talk in the Basel dialect. How else are we supposed to communicate?"

"Well, that's men for you. Always trying to lay down the law," observed Hunkeler.

"You can talk. You're retired and can take things easy."

He didn't reply to that.

"Have I offended you?" she asked, after a moment of silence.

"No. And anyway, you're right."

"Sorry. Come on, let's drink to being here."

They clinked their glasses.

"So how are you doing, old man?"

"I gave a lift to Christian Moor, the painter," he told her. "He was hitchhiking in Hésingue."

"The guy with the grey-and-white paintings?"

"Yes, him. He said people no longer have time to listen, he said it was the illness of our time."

"Where was he going?"

"To the inn at Knoeringue."

She broke off a piece of the baguette. "Wonderful," she commented. "It always reminds me of Paris when I tear off a piece of baguette. Anyway, you're one of the few people I know who are really good at listening. It's because you're able to be in the moment. I think that's one of the main reasons I love you. You're inquisitive. But why did Moor want to go to the Knoeringue inn?"

"He set fire to his paintings. So they sent him to the Friedmatt, and now he's run away."

"Oh my goodness. Men are just hopeless at growing old."

Hunkeler said nothing.

Hedwig looked him in the eye, a cool and measured gaze. "Hey, you look properly depressed," she observed.

"Nonsense."

"Not nonsense, I can see it in your face. Tell me, what's been going on?"

"Nothing."

"Don't give me that. How can I listen if you won't talk to me? Come on, have another glass." She topped him up.

"OK. But it'll take a while."

"The night is still young, the morning's a long way off."

"Over the past few days and nights I've been thinking back on things," he told her. "I've been wondering what exactly I've done in my life that's worth mentioning.

"In Hésingue, on the edge of the village, there's that small farmhouse with the projecting roof. When I was seventeen, I waited there with my friend Anton for six hours for someone to give us a lift. Our plan was to hitchhike to Paris. On the first day we got as far as Vesoul. When night fell, we walked a few steps away from the road and slept in a meadow. In the morning we went and stood by the road again. By evening we'd reached a suburb of Paris. We had the address of a youth hostel in the south of the city, in Malakoff. We walked there. It took three hours. We arrived at midnight, but all we found was a giant building site. We sat down on a bench

37

and ate the rest of a loaf of bread. Then one of those black, low-slung Citroëns stopped beside us. A young police officer got out and asked us what we were doing there. 'Waiting,' we replied. 'Get in,' he said. They drove us around the area for half an hour, completing their usual patrol. Then we stopped outside a police station and went in. The young *flic* opened a cell and gave us two woolly blankets. We fell asleep instantly.

"In the morning we were woken by the smell of coffee. They invited us to sit down at their table, we had *café au lait* and a croissant each. *Bonne chance!* the *flic* said to us, and off we trotted."

"And that's making you feel depressed?" Hedwig asked. "Why? It's a lovely story."

"It carries on," he replied. "And it gets even more lovely. Late that evening we found another youth hostel in the centre of Paris. It was overcrowded. I hung my jacket up on a wall, with my passport and the money I'd saved up for the trip in it. That's how carefree, how naive I was. We slept on the floor. When I put my jacket on in the morning, I noticed that my money had gone. The passport was still there. We deliberated and came to the conclusion that the money Anton had with him wouldn't be enough for a week in Paris. But it would be enough for both of us to hitchhike to the sea.

"We stayed in Paris another night, went up the Eiffel Tower and visited the Louvre and Montmartre. Then we hitched to Normandy, to Cherbourg. We looked at the port and the sea and collected shells on the beach. Then we hitchhiked all the way across France, back towards Basel. On the way we visited the cathedral at Chartres. At night we found shelter on farms, sleeping in the stables or the barn. In most places, they gave us bread in the evening and a mug of milk in the morning.

"Once, the farmer led us into the cowshed, to a pen for calves. She wished us good night and went back to the farmhouse. We thought we'd have to bed down without eating anything. But then a teenage girl came in with a tray. On the tray were bread and cheese, a jug of water and a jug of wine. But the loveliest thing about it all was the girl. We stared at her and she stared at us.

"When I pass that house in Hésingue I often remember that trip to Paris. How immune I was to everything back then, how unassailable. Even though I absorbed everything that could be absorbed. I knew nothing would happen to me. I also knew that this journey was meant for me. For no one else, just for me.

"When I saw the old guy standing there this morning, it gave me a shock. He was the picture of misery. He looked like someone who's trying to obliterate his tracks. Dosed up on psychotropic drugs, marked by too much red wine. His house sold, his life's work turned to ashes. He'll be glad to find some company with the landlady in Knoeringue."

"And you think something similar could happen to you?"

Hunkeler didn't reply.

"What a load of rubbish. You've got me. You've got your pension and this house. Being in hospital has made you depressed. The anaesthetic, the interference with your body. You need to recover from that. By the way, the story you've just told me is really nice."

"When I was in hospital I could never get to sleep at night," he told her. "I rang the bell and a night nurse would come and give me a sleeping pill. A young, attractive woman with brown eyes. On the third night, a woman with green-grey eyes came. She smelled of cinnamon, otherwise she looked the same. She gave me the pill, and waited until it had started to work. Then she went over to the guy next to me, Fankhauser, and stuck a needle in his belly. She watched wordlessly as he started to wheeze and gasp for air. It was as if I was paralysed. Then sleep overcame me. The next morning I heard that Fankhauser had died."

Hunkeler saw the look of shock on Hedwig's face.

"He was terminally ill though," she said. "You could see that he was going to die soon."

"Still. If what I saw really happened, then it was a pre-meditated killing. So murder."

"But why? Perhaps she wanted to release him from his suffering."

"No, she was too ruthless for that. She did it like someone who was exacting revenge."

"How can you know that? Perhaps the pill you took contained morphine and you were hallucinating. Are you even sure it was a different nurse to the other nights?"

"She had different eyes. She smelled different. She wore a different ring."

"You can change your perfume. And your ring."

Hedwig got up, fetched a second bottle and opened it slowly. He could tell she was looking for an alternative explanation. She almost always found one.

"Have some more wine. Otherwise you won't be able to sleep."

He drank and she topped up his glass.

"It was a dream," Hedwig decided. "A terrible, nightmarish fantasy. Surely you're not going to saddle yourself with an imagined murder case, you're supposed to be recuperating. It was a blessing for Fankhauser that he could die. Forget him, let him go. And forget about old Moor. He's just a frustrated artist who's past his prime. Think of your trip to Paris instead. Of the shells you collected on the beach at Cherbourg."

The next morning Hunkeler woke up early. He was in Hedwig's bed. He could feel her hand on the back of his head, her breath on his neck. He could also feel the wine, he'd drunk too much. But he'd slept well. He could hear Fritz the cockerel outside, crowing at the coming dawn.

Hunkeler got up and went over to the open window. The first light was creeping across the snow-covered lawn. The sky was clear. He could hear a faint chirruping coming from the pear tree. He looked closely. Yes, it was a black redstart. There it sat with its dark gleaming chest, newly arrived after migrating back from its winter quarters in the south.

On Saturday, 22 March, Hunkeler was sitting on a pew in Basel Minster, listening to the words of Dr Albert Debrunner, former councillor of the Liberal Party, who was giving the eulogy for Dr Fankhauser. It was an illustrious event, the Minster was packed.

Hunkeler had caught a cold during the chilly days in Alsace and his nose was terribly blocked. He pulled out his handkerchief, spread it out and blew into it. The sound that came out was akin to a trumpet blast, and was evidently perceived as disruptive. Not that anybody turned their head, there was no hissing or whispering. That wasn't the done thing here in Basel, it would have been considered vulgar. But the indignation was palpable. Up in the pulpit, Dr Debrunner fell silent. He crossly looked around the congregation of mourners, trying to spot the culprit, and Hunkeler froze.

"An irreplaceable loss for our city," Debrunner said, taking up the thread again. "Dr Fankhauser leaves behind a hole no one can fill. This is the mark of all great men, that they are unique and irreproducible. All we can do is bow down before the deceased, in sincere gratitude. We will use all our power and wisdom to ward off the attacks on our city and keep alight the torch he so valiantly carried."

These were the closing words of the speech. Hunkeler found himself gripped by an irrepressible urge to sneeze. He yanked his handkerchief back out and clamped it round his nose. Again he felt the indignation rising around him. He held his breath with all the force he could muster.

At that moment, the organ burst forth. The mighty bass notes filled the lofty space and sent a tremble through the souls of the congregation. Hunkeler sneezed loudly, three times in a row. It was unavoidable, there was nothing he could do. Then he blew his nose and tucked away his handkerchief again. With relief he listened to the sound emanating from those enormous pipes high up on the back wall of the nave. It was a fugue of some sort, from the baroque period. He liked it.

The first to rise below the pulpit at the front was the divorcee, Sabine Fankhauser-Wackernagel. She stepped towards the altar and silently took a bow in front of the casket that stood there surrounded by red roses. There were no other bouquets or wreaths. *Commemorative donations should kindly be made to the Cancer League*, the death announcement had stated.

42

Hunkeler had expected to see Ms Fankhauser-Wackernagel accompanied by the son Fankhauser had told him about. But apparently he wasn't here.

Debrunner approached the woman and waited patiently until she turned away from the altar. He took her hand and stood stony-faced when she momentarily leaned against him with surprising tenderness, as if expecting help from him. A little too intimate, was the general observation among those present. But again the sound of the organ rose to a powerful crescendo and flushed away all misgivings.

Hunkeler remained sitting for several minutes. He couldn't have left his pew anyway, there were far too many people. Fankhauser had been a prominent personality. Born into humble circumstances, as Debrunner had informed them, Fankhauser had grown up in Riehen, where his father was a border guard. He'd gone on to study, entering a turbulent time of revolutionary activism as a follower of Marx and Ho Chi Minh – "all down to the exuberant temperament of youth, naturally". Here Debrunner had ventured a smile. Following his graduation in law, Fankhauser had soon found his way back down to reality and settled on a career at the Basel Volksbank, Debrunner had reassured the listeners. And later, as its director, Fankhauser had steadfastly defended the Volksbank during difficult times, "when the bank was subject to ruthless attacks from abroad".

Now the dignitaries were beginning to parade along the nave, led by Dr Schmidlin with Sabine Fankhauser on his arm. Schmidlin occupied the newly created post of city mayor, chiefly by interfering in every kind of cultural issue. For Basel was a city of culture. Anyone with a certain social standing was culturally active, even if this merely consisted of vociferously questioning what exactly constituted culture.

The bigwigs of Basel got in line behind Schmidlin, including a small number of women. First came the politicians, well-known faces from every party, slowly walking towards the exit with appropriately restrained grief. Behind them the leaders of the city's cultural institutions, a few pharmaceutical industry managers and some honourable aged men from the banking sector, accompanied by their black-veiled wives. They were rarely to be seen in public, except during Carnival, when they drummed and piped their way along the streets of Basel. But then they were in full costume and masked.

Hunkeler recognized almost all of these ladies and gents. He didn't know them privately, only by sight. And only because, sooner or later, people's paths crossed. It was precisely because Basel was a purely urban city, with no back-country, that it functioned like a village in which the old, established families secretly pulled all the strings. An incomer from Aargau, such as Hunkeler was, would never find out how those strings were connected. Nor did he want to.

When his pew had emptied he filed out into the left aisle and walked to the front to look at the Romanesque relief. It depicted the martyrdom of Vincent of Saragossa. There were four stations, ending with the saint's death at the stake. It was the most illustrious artwork in the entire Minster, apart from the golden altar frontal donated by Henry II, which the city of Basel had foolishly sold to the Musée de Cluny in Paris some years after gaining independence in 1833.

Antoinette Oser, leader of the Liberal faction in the cantonal parliament, stood in front of the relief. She was engaged in a whispered conversation with two men who, judging by their accents, came from Zurich. Hunkeler listened as she pointed at one of the stone ravens and explained that the carrion birds were waiting for the corpse, in order to devour it.

"Actually," Hunkeler interrupted, "you're mistaken. The ravens aren't waiting to devour the corpse. They're sacred to Vincent and are protecting his soul."

His comment was met with a venomous glare sharp enough to skewer him.

He walked on and watched as a man lifted the casket onto a small trolley and took it away. Only the roses remained. They exuded a curiously morbid scent. The organist up in the gallery played on, the booming sound of the pipes proclaiming the omnipotence of a punitive God. Hunkeler enjoyed surrendering to this kind of music. He was quite partial to theatrical things, even though he had long stopped going to actual theatres. But here, standing in the transept of the old building, he took pleasure in the little concert. It was strange, he thought, how these architectural relics of Christian faith and Christian money had endured throughout the centuries, from Constance to Basel, from Freiburg and Strasbourg all the way down to Cologne. They had withstood the incursions of the Huns, the Reformation and the bombs of the Second World War. And even today, in an era when the powerful had long ceased to make use of the Cross to advance their interests, it was still the done thing to flock to a Christian temple to pay one's last respects to one of those powerful people.

The Minster was an awe-inspiring space, rising high like a beech forest, with a cross-ribbed vault that arched across the soaring expanse. Up there, in the gallery above the pulpit, a petite female figure now appeared, seemingly out of thin air. She was wearing a pale garment, her hair concealed by a blue headscarf. She stood motionlessly, taking in the entire space, from the rosette above the organ to the coloured windows of the chancel. Then she raised her right hand in a slow, blessing sort of gesture.

Hunkeler looked around. The Minster had emptied, he was standing there alone. Only the organ could be heard, its sound swelling to a closing crescendo.

He looked back up. The figure had vanished.


The wake took place at the Restaurant Kunsthalle, in the more elegant part where white tablecloths and crystal glasses set the tone. Hunkeler spotted Inspector Madörin and Police Corporal Lüdi at a table right by the entrance. Madörin, wearing a grim expression, had positioned himself so as to have a good view of the room. The guests had evidently lost no time in indulging in the wine – a Pinot Noir from the Markgräflerland just across the Rhine, where the city of Basel owned a vineyard. People appeared to be in high spirits, they were shaking hands and slapping each other on their black-suited shoulders. High-pitched laughter from some of the more inebriated women intermittently cut through the general noise.

"Don't you dare come and interfere," Madörin hissed as Hunkeler sat down at his table. "You have no business being here."

"This is the wake for the venerable Dr Fankhauser, also known as Red Steff," replied Hunkeler. "I shared a hospital room with him during his final days. I'm here to pay my respects. And what brings you here?"

Madörin glared at him, apparently fighting the urge to wring his former boss's neck.

"Steady," Lüdi said sharply. "We're at the Kunsthalle, not at the station."

"He needs to keep his fingers out of this," Madörin snarled.

"Out of what?" Hunkeler asked.

Dr Debrunner walked past hurriedly, apparently heading for the toilets. He was wearing his TV face, the soft, all-knowing smile that had served him so well on his journey to the top. He briefly stopped beside them. "Well look at this, the police are here too," he said. "To what do we owe the pleasure?"

"We're mourning too," Madörin informed him. "Indeed a great loss for Basel. And I'd like to speak to you briefly. If you could spare us a moment?"

"That's impossible, I'm afraid," Debrunner replied regretfully while maintaining his smile. "If you have questions, please get in touch with my office." And then he was gone.

Abdul, long-standing *chef de service* at the Kunsthalle, brought over three plates of cold meat and poured the wine. He nodded at Hunkeler with reserved politeness.

"Cheers everyone," said Hunkeler and took a sip. "Tastes fantastic, like a good Burgundy wine. This comes from an excellent location on the Isteiner ridge. Dry terrain, and I've heard it's now been declared a conservation area, due to the almost Mediterranean flora. It must be said, Basel folk know a good thing when they see it. And if it isn't theirs already, they buy it."

Hunkeler popped a piece of roast veal into his mouth.

"Superb," he commented. "Life in the tri-border area is good when you have a generous pension. Alsace,

Markgräflerland and Basel, they go together well. And everywhere they speak the beautiful, old Alemannic dialect. If only one didn't have to work, wouldn't you agree? All the stress. If only one wasn't continuously being lambasted from above in this beautiful city."

Madörin didn't say a word. He was close to exploding, but he didn't dare.

"A sudden death," Hunkeler continued. "He was terminally ill, of course, but it was surprising nevertheless. Was it the insulin? An unexpected cardiac arrest? Did they perform an autopsy? And if not, then why not?"

Madörin pushed away his plate. With some effort, he swallowed what was in his mouth. He didn't seem to be enjoying it. Then he stood up, stony-faced, and walked out.

"You shouldn't have done that," said Lüdi.

Hunkeler topped up his glass and drank. Truly like a good Burgundy, only a fraction drier, which he liked. "I just don't like the guy," he said. "He is and always will be a mean bastard."

"That's quite possible," Lüdi conceded. "But he's a good investigator. And he doesn't give up so easily."

"Why does he have to be so rude? Why can't he simply shake my hand and ask me how I'm doing? Anyway, what's the story with the autopsy?"

"There was no autopsy. Even though Madörin requested one."

"Isn't that a bit unusual?" Hunkeler commented. "With such a significant figure people generally want to know exactly what they died of."

"Heart failure, according to the report. The body was disposed of very quickly."

"Seems like someone was in a hurry. I wonder why?"

Lüdi briefly fell silent. Then he said it anyway.

"Madörin thinks it was on the orders of someone at the very top."

"What do you mean, the very top?"

"From Debrunner, for example," said Lüdi. "He was also involved with the leftist student group during his time at university, like Fankhauser."

"Back then almost everyone was. Certainly as sympathizers, at least."

"Madörin suspects a conspiracy, as per usual. He says they're trying to sweep something under the carpet that should rightly be laid on the table. He's hopping mad because he keeps being stonewalled everywhere. Even by Prosecutor Suter."

"Well I never, how odd. Basel's elite doesn't want to be reminded of their youthful follies. Why ever not?" Hunkeler wondered.

"Because those youthful follies were meticulously recorded at the time and could easily be made public. By the *Basler Zeitung* for example, which is of course no longer a left-liberal newspaper. Since the sell-off, it's swung to the right. But why do you ask? You already know all of this."

"I ask because I want to know what Fankhauser died of. What's your opinion, anyway?"

"I have no opinion whatsoever. And anyway, I shouldn't really be talking to you about it."

"OK. But your private number is still the same?"

Lüdi hesitated. Then he nodded.

\*

A while later Hunkeler moved to a table where he'd spotted a couple of acquaintances from the old days.

By now, the noise had reached an impressive level. The deep laughter of the men had grown to a roar and the screeching from the women had become even more piercing. Basel's high society was in no way averse to the delights of good wine. They just needed a sound reason to indulge in those delights. The wake in honour of an eminent fellow citizen was evidently reason enough.

He sat down beside two authors, Schubiger and Bikle, and Paul Egloff, whom Hunkeler liked. Egloff had studied philosophy and subsequently worked as an editor at various newspapers. He'd always remained faithful to his left-wing convictions and consequently kept getting into quarrels with his chief editors, all of whom were also left-leaning, but only to a certain extent – which was determined by the newspapers' owners. Eventually, Egloff had grown tired of journalism and become a carpenter in a cooperative of craftspeople.

Schubiger and Bikle had both devoted their writing skills to the cause of the revolutionary proletariat and had joined the Communist Party in the seventies. Bikle had written voluminous novels about his upper-class origins that were celebrated by the critics and ignored by the reading public because they were deadly boring. Schubiger had published political poetry intended to rouse the working classes. He'd signed every leftist petition available, against the Vietnam War, the neutron bomb and nuclear power stations. But even that hadn't increased his book sales.

Bikle, who came from a stinking rich family of academics, was evidently doing better than Schubiger. He was dressed in fine English cloth, while Schubiger sat there like a sad migratory bird that had missed the departure south.

"What gives us the honour?" Bikle asked.

"The longing for human kindness and warmth, the memory of old times," replied Hunkeler.

"I don't normally share a table with the police," Bikle commented. "But I'll make an exception, since we're at a wake."

"Glad to hear it. Can I have some wine?"

Hunkeler poured himself a glass.

"Cheers, everyone. Here's to Red Steff."

They raised their glasses.

"Deserted to the class enemy," said Schubiger. "How inconsistent, how shameful. What happened to class awareness?"

"Do you mean me?" Hunkeler asked.

"Yes, you too."

"Not true. My political views haven't changed much." He looked at Bikle. "How are the shares doing?"

"Not bad, thank you. The only way to fight capitalism is with capital. That's my sad realization."

"Fankhauser was a miserable opportunist," Schubiger insisted. "Just like Debrunner. If you give capitalism a finger it'll take the whole hand. That's why I've always kept away from big money."

"And the small money? Do you take that?" Hunkeler asked.

That made Schubiger laugh. It was a hoarse cackle from a dry throat.

"You may scoff, and you're right of course. But look at Debrunner's table. Look how he's sucking up to Frau

51

Sarasin. And he once wanted to bring about the revolution. It's disgusting."

As if to confirm, Debrunner's group burst into shrieks of laughter, presumably in response to a dirty joke.

"It's sad what's become of us," said Schubiger.

"True," Bikle agreed. "But that's what time does. It gnaws away at you until you become as smooth as a pebble on the bed of the Rhine."

"There's nothing wrong with the pebbles in the Rhine," said Egloff. He still wore his hair in a long plait, which had become hopelessly tangled and matted over the years.

They nodded. They laughed. It was true. They were a pretty dilapidated bunch.

"It's surprising to see what's become of the revolutionary youth of old," Egloff commented. "The red–green coalition has a majority in this city, and would have the power to rule. But they don't rule, they merely administrate. Political discussions revolve around what time a tradesperson can drive into the centre, which stretches of the Rhine dogs are allowed to swim in, and whether we should put the rubbish bags outside our houses or take them to collection points. And the traffic problem is resolved by telling drivers to have their lights on during the day. That's what counts for politics in Basel, it's a joke. The important questions are decided by the pharmaceutical industry, because that's where Basel gets all its money from to pay for everything. Democracy has surrendered because industry knows no democracy."

Hunkeler disagreed. "I think Basel is a pleasant city to live in. A moderate climate, clean water, forests close by. And nobody has to go hungry."

"And all of it funded by the pharmaceutical companies,"

countered Egloff. "The only god humankind still believes in. Chemical formulas have replaced confessions of faith, pills have replaced communion."

"Still a socialist then?" Hunkeler asked.

"No, anarchist."

"Not easy in the era of the internet. What do you get up to? Where do you live?"

"Currently in a trailer on the campsite in Huningue. Sometimes I work as a chef at the Alte Grenze. I never pay any bills, as a matter of principle. Most of the time they don't even know where I live. Do you have a mobile phone?"

"Yes."

"Throw it away. It'll give you nothing but trouble."

"And living this way, does it work?"

"Yes, if you're prepared to spend time inside every now and then. I always go in winter. I've never known a prison not to be heated. But you have to like your own company."

Hunkeler wondered whether he liked his own company. Whether that was enough for him. Probably not, he thought. He needed people, he needed Hedwig. He was about to answer in that vein when he saw some people saying good-bye and leaving. Among them was a petite woman wearing a pale outfit and a blue headscarf. She was walking beside a man, their arms hooked.

"You'll have to excuse me," said Hunkeler and stood up. He followed the group outside and down Steinenberg Strasse to Barfüsserplatz. All he could see of the woman was her back and the headscarf. But he felt certain. He caught up with her, grabbed her by the arm and pulled her round. He was looking into a face he'd never seen before.

"What on earth do you think you're doing?" the man beside her asked. "Have you gone mad?"

Hunkeler looked again, more closely now. It wasn't her, there was no doubt.

"I'm so sorry, my mistake. I feel terribly embarrassed. I beg your pardon."

The man was furious. "Do you have some kind of problem with headscarves? Shall I call the police?"

"No, not at all. I thought I knew her. I was wrong."

Hunkeler walked away as quickly as he could and turned into the narrow alleyway that led up Leonhardsberg. He realized he was shaking with agitation. What was the matter with him? Was he suffering from paranoia or delusions?

The following morning he woke up in his bed in Alsace. He could feel the two cats against the backs of his knees. He reached round for them and they began to purr. Cold air was coming in through the open window, a blackbird was singing outside. It was probably sitting on the roof of the pigsty, like most mornings.

He heard the phone ring in the hallway. He waited to see if the ringing would stop. When it didn't, he got up and answered. "What's up?" he asked.

It was Lüdi.

"Sorry to wake you. But it's ten o'clock and high time you had some breakfast."

There was a laugh, which sounded more like a snigger.

"Go on," Hunkeler urged. "Fire away. I'm standing in the hallway dressed in a nightshirt and my feet are getting cold."

"Dr Debrunner was struck down. Yesterday, shortly before midnight."

"Struck down, how?"

"With a hard object on the head. He has a fractured skull and is in intensive care. He left the Kunsthalle around 11 p.m. and took a tram to Bruderholz, where he lives. A hundred yards from his house he was struck down from behind."

"Didn't he try to defend himself?"

"It seems he didn't hear the attacker. He'd probably had a fair amount to drink."

"Was he mugged?"

"No. His ID, money and phone were still there."

"Wait a moment," said Hunkeler. "I need to think."

He went to the kitchen, poured himself a glass of water and drank it slowly. He could feel the cold in the back of his head. It was creeping down into his guts.

"Why are you telling me?" Hunkeler asked Lüdi when he was back on the phone. "I'm retired, I don't need to know any of this."

More sniggering, which didn't bode well.

"Prosecutor Suter thinks we should consult you, because you're the same age as Debrunner and you're familiar with people of that generation."

"And how does Madörin feel about that?"

"He's seething with anger."

"Let him seethe. Meanwhile I'm enjoying my retirement. Do you know what I'm going to do now? First, I'm going to let the hens out and check whether one of them has laid an egg. If yes, then I'll have it for breakfast. And I'll have a big pot of tea with it. Then I'm going for a long walk."

"What shall I tell Suter?"

"Tell him if he wants something from me, he should call me. He has my number."

A little later Hunkeler was sitting at the kitchen table, looking out at the garden, at the cherry tree, the willow, the pear tree and the poplar. The sun was halfway up in the sky. The primroses had burst into flower, delicate yellow splodges of colour in the emerging green.

He pulled on his boots and set out along the stream, which was in full spate. He walked past the sawmill compound and took in the scent of the freshly sawed wood, boards of varying thickness and size, oak, beech, wild cherry, stacked ten feet high. Next to it stood the house of the sawmill owner, built using the beams of demolished half-timbered houses.

There were no stone buildings in this area, apart from the old church in Knoeringue. This was because the limestone had to be carted in from dozens of miles away. People used what was available locally. Wood and clay.

He walked up to the top of the rise, taking it steady. Hedwig had advised him not to overdo it. She'd told him to take his age into account. But how did one take one's age into account? By lying in bed and waiting for death? Hell no. Humans were flight animals. They had to stay on the move, on and on. That's what kept them alive, until it struck them down. But for now he was still on his feet. He increased his pace until he got out of breath. He sucked the fresh air deep into his lungs, it felt great.

Up on the high plain there was still snow on the ground in places. The white crust was pierced by the brown, decaying stumps of the old maize stalks. An all-encompassing, almost sad stillness hung over the fields. Soon tractors with man-high wheels would drive across them and tear the earth open again with their ploughshares.

Up ahead at the forest's edge he saw a huntsman standing beside the old oak, a rifle draped across his arm. It was Philipp Meierhans, a former investment banker at the Basel Volksbank, now retired. From what Hunkeler had heard, he'd bought the house of the old artist Moor. Presumably he was waiting for a young boar roaming in search of new territory, hoping to slay it with a shot to the heart.

Hunkeler briefly waved at Meierhans and then disappeared into the woods. He didn't like hunters, even though he knew there were too many wild boar in these parts.

It was a bare woodland that surrounded him now. No spruce or firs grew here and the beeches and oaks hadn't come into leaf yet. It was a primeval forest, largely unexploited. There were no walking trails, nobody came to hike here. He was more likely to encounter a wild boar.

In the afternoon, Hunkeler lay on his bed and read about the First World War. He read about a battle in Sudan in the year 1898, when the British used machine guns on a large scale for the first time in history. The Brits were fighting an army of 50,000 Sudanese and mowed around half that number down as they came charging towards them. The British side had lost forty-eight men. It was clear from that point that an attacker didn't stand a chance against machine guns, no matter how brave he was. Yet in the First World War they had carried on attacking as if the rules of the cavalry charge still applied. Trench warfare had set in around the Somme and the Marne, during the course of which millions of young men were sent to their deaths.

It was all such a long time ago, thought Hunkeler as he was reading that. And since surpassed by the Second World War, which was even more terrible. But then he remembered that his father had been nine years old when the First World War broke out. And suddenly it didn't seem so long ago.

In the evening he went across to the cowshed of the farm next door. He sat down on the bench and watched the woman do the milking. She kept three cows. She fed the milk to the calves and pigs.

Being in this shed always gave Hunkeler a feeling of timelessness. It was like something from the Old Testament, the slow munching and chewing, the warmth emanating from the animals' bodies, as if nothing in the world could go adrift. "Thank you for looking after the hens," he said.

"*Merci* for the eggs," she replied.

It was always like this when he was away. If Hunkeler's car wasn't parked in front of the house, his neighbour took care of the hens.

He watched as she removed the teat cups from one cow and attached them to the udders of the next one. He liked the way she did it, with measured, precise movements. He knew that the cows didn't produce much milk, they weren't given supplementary feed, just grass and hay. He also knew that her husband had been in the hospital at Altkirch for weeks.

"Someone came by," she said. "*Il est venu à midi.* At midday, when you were out. He knocked on your door. I told him you'd gone out for a walk. He walked round your house once, as if he was looking for something. Then he wandered off towards the forest."

"What did he look like? Was he wearing a red jacket?"

"*Oui*, an older gentleman."

"That must have been Moor, the painter. I've heard he now lives at the Stollers' in Knoeringue."

"People say he's hiding," she told him. "*Très drôle*, it's a bit strange."

"I know him," Hunkeler replied. "He probably wanted to pay me a visit. He's harmless. He was in the Friedmatt psychiatric clinic and ran away."

"*Il est fou?* Is he crazy?"

"No, more depressed than anything. He told me he didn't want to swallow all those pills any more."

"*Ça, je comprends*, I understand that. These days the doctors want to cure everything with pills. Even though they don't address the cause, *n'est-ce pas?* Wouldn't you agree, Monsieur?"

She looked at him with worried eyes, and he knew she was talking about her husband.

"Monsieur Moor, isn't he the one who sold the house in Knoeringue? On Römerstrasse. A lovely old house. *Pourquoi?* Why did he sell it?"

"Perhaps because he needed money. As an artist, I imagine he only has a state pension. He can't live off that."

She removed the teat cups and switched off the machine.

"*En Alsace* he can live off it like a bee in clover." She poured the contents of the milk churn into two buckets, one for each calf.

"Do you know when the big bunkers were built?" he asked her. "The ones over by Helfrantzkirch and Folgensbourg. Was that during the First World War?"

"*Mais non.* In the first war, Alsace belonged to Germany. The bunkers all face the Rhine, *gäge s'Düütsche*, towards

Germany. So during the Second World War. *Pourquoi?* Why do you ask?"

"Because I'm reading a book about the First World War."

"*Ah, oui?* That's a hundred years ago now, *n'est-ce pas?* Why are you reading about that? Switzerland was spared."

"Because I want to understand how it all came about."

"Here in Alsace people only want one thing. They want to forget. But I have a book about the First World War too. It's by an Alsatian from St Ulrich, a village between Altkirch and Belfort. Do you want to read it?"

"Yes please."

"*D'accord*, I'll fetch it when I've finished with the animals."

The book was called *The Kaiser's Reluctant Conscript* and was written by a farmer called Dominik Richert. He had served on the German side from 1914 to 1918, first in Alsace, then in Flanders, the Carpathians and in Russia. When he was posted back to the Western Front in March 1918, he deserted to the French forces. After the war, he wrote down everything he'd experienced as a common soldier, then he put the manuscript in the attic. Decades later it was discovered there, deciphered and published. All of this Hunkeler learned from the postscript. And he looked forward to reading it.

The next morning Hunkeler rang his old friend Lukas, a general physician in Basel, and asked him for an appointment. They arranged to meet in the afternoon.

Lukas' medical practice was located in a retirement complex.

"What can I help you with?" Lukas asked as Hunkeler entered. "How did the operation go?"

"Good. Everyone is telling me I'm doing well, and the doctors are happy with me."

"And you, are you happy?"

"Yesterday I was out walking for three hours. That went quite well."

"And what brings you here?"

"I'm not sure. I'd like a check-up. Can you have a listen to my chest?"

"OK, undress your top half."

Hunkeler did as asked. Lukas listened to his lungs and then took his blood pressure.

"All fine. Anything else?"

"Yes. The thing is, I'm wondering whether I'm suffering from hallucinations," Hunkeler confessed. "The night nurse at the hospital gave me a sleeping pill every night. I always fell asleep immediately. Now I'd like to know whether it was morphine. And I'd like to know if it was the same night nurse throughout."

"Didn't you ask?"

"I did. But I'm not convinced."

"OK, that shouldn't be a problem. Hang on." Lukas dialled a number and was apparently on the phone to a colleague at the Merian Iselin Hospital. "The nurse is called Lydia Siegenthaler," he said after putting the phone down. "She was on night duty the whole week. The pill contained a morphine-like substance. It's quite possible for someone to experience mild hallucinations after taking it. But only briefly, people generally fall asleep very quickly. Why do you want to know?"

Hunkeler looked out the window onto the park, where some old men were sitting on a bench enjoying the spring sunshine. "I'm wondering whether I'm going crazy," he said. "At the hospital, I was in the bed next to Stephan Fankhauser. I'm sure you've heard that he died. As far as I know, no autopsy was carried out."

Lukas nodded, but didn't say anything.

"The night he died, I rang for the nurse shortly after midnight. The nurse that came looked similar to the one from the night before. But I'm almost certain this was a different person. Different eyes, different scent. She gave me the pill. She waited a while. Then she gave Fankhauser an injection, even though he tried to defend himself. She watched as he started to gasp for air. Then I fell asleep."

They were now both looking out at the old men. It was a nice scene.

"Perhaps insulin," Lukas commented. "That can cause agonal gasping. If what you're telling me is true. Perhaps you were just dreaming."

"They both wore a blue headscarf. Yesterday, after Fankhauser's memorial ceremony at the Minster, I saw a similar-looking person, also with a blue headscarf, high up above the side aisle. I only saw her briefly. When I looked back up she was gone. Afterwards, at the wake in the Kunsthalle, I again saw a similar-looking woman. I only saw her from behind as she was leaving. I ran after her and pulled her by the arm. She was completely unknown to me."

"Red Steff, the phony revolutionary," said Lukas. "I never liked him. He advocated for an armed struggle against capitalism."

The bench outside was now in the shade. The old men gathered themselves up to limp back inside.

"And now you're wondering whether it was all a hallucination?"

"Yes."

"Theoretically, this kind of drug can cause all sorts of issues, including prolonged cognitive disturbances. I very much hope this is the case. If not, it would be a matter for the police. Wouldn't it?"

"I don't know," Hunkeler replied.

The weather was poor the following days. There was a steady rain, the kind typical for southern Alsace. The Atlantic clouds rushed eastwards unhindered, through the Belfort Gap, and swamped everything – pastures and fields and the deep tracks left by tractors in the forest.

Hunkeler spent most of the time lying on his bed, with the gentle crackle from the stove in his ears and the two cats by his feet. He read about the First World War.

He didn't have a newspaper subscription. In Basel he always read the daily *Basler Zeitung*. Everybody did this, even though they moaned about it. Here in Alsace he was happy to do without. He listened to Basel's local radio station in the evenings and if he was having a coffee in Knoeringue he read the *Dernières Nouvelles*.

Hunkeler hadn't heard anything new about Debrunner, except that his condition was stable and that the investigation had been accorded the highest priority. This meant either that his colleagues at Waaghof station hadn't found anything out yet, or that they couldn't or wouldn't say. Hunkeler suspected it was the former. Over the years, he had dealt with the most bizarre crimes in which people were randomly attacked and injured for no apparent reason. The perpetrators made off, soft-footed and swift, without any attempt at robbery. As there was no discernible motive, the CID had no angle on the investigation. The crimes remained inexplicable, appalling and frightening. The only difference in the Debrunner case was that the offence had taken place in the Bruderholz district, where nothing of this kind had ever happened. And the fact that a well-known Basel politician was involved.

He turned over a page in Dominik Richert's book and carried on reading about the trench warfare between the Germans and the French. "*A little to the right of my shooting position was a German soldier lying face down, with his head towards me. His helmet had come off when he fell. As a result of putrefaction, the skin with the hair had slid down and a hand-sized area of his skull was visible, bleached by the rain and the sun. In one hand he was still holding the rusty rifle with its bayonet. The flesh of his fingers had already rotted away and the knuckles were sticking out. It was very eerie, seeing the white skull in front of me, especially at night.*"

It struck Hunkeler as somewhat perverse that he was listening to the cats purring while reading such sentences. But he'd been seized by a curiosity to know what it had been like for a soldier back then. Dominik Richert was a reliable witness. He had fought in the war because he had to, not because he felt passionate about his country. His home was southern Alsace, not Germany or France. He had no reason to be on the banks of the Marne or in Russia. And he wrote from the viewpoint of an ordinary, rational person, which was rare. People like that didn't generally write books.

*"Bravery, heroism – do they exist?"* the farmer Richert asked himself. *"I doubt it very much, for all I saw when we were under fire was fear, trepidation and desperation written in every face. There was no sign of bravery, courage and the like. In reality it is only the terrible discipline, the compulsion, that drives the soldier forward and to his death."*

In the evening, Hedwig arrived. They drove to Tagsdorf near Altkirch, where Madame Chappuis ran a classy eatery at the old Adler. She had set her mind on turning the former village public house into a gourmet establishment. Her husband cooked a four-course menu every day while she served the customers.

Parked in front of the building was an Italian luxury car with a Basel licence plate. A display announced today's menu: *Consommé de légumes*, leaf salad, roast veal with morel mushrooms, and profiteroles for dessert.

When they stepped inside, the place was almost empty, as usual. Only the table in the corner at the back was occupied. It was the investment banker Meierhans, in the company of a younger woman.

Hunkeler went to sit down at a table by the door, but Meierhans had already spotted him. "Look who's here, it's Hunkeler," he called across the room. "I've been wanting to catch up with you for some time. Come over here, come and join us. After all, we were fellow students back in the day. May I introduce you to my fiancée?"

Polite as Hunkeler was, he first helped Hedwig out of her coat and then went to the back to shake hands with

Meierhans and his fiancée. "Pleased to meet you," he said curtly.

"Why so surly? We're in a top-class restaurant, the Côte de Beaune is excellent. And everything at a reasonable price. Bring your wife over, have a glass with us."

"Not today," said Hunkeler. "Another time perhaps."

But Meierhans was on a roll, probably fuelled by the wine. "Have you heard anything new about Debrunner?" he said. "It's appalling. Struck down, just like that. And up in the peaceful Bruderholz district, of all places. Is there anywhere that's safe these days? It won't be long before it all kicks off here in Alsace too, you wait. And what's the Basel police been doing all this time? Dragging its feet, it seems. Come on, get your act together, Inspector Hunkeler. Otherwise anarchy will take over."

"Oh, Philipp," the woman interjected. Her voice sounded friendly and warm. "Don't get so worked up. You can see he doesn't want to chat."

"We're celebrating a special occasion," said Hunkeler and tried to smile. "A tête-à-tête, so to speak. We want to enjoy a quiet meal, just the two of us."

"Aha, a wedding anniversary, is it?"

"Yes, that kind of thing."

"Well in that case, many congratulations. By the way, what is that artist Moor doing, sitting in the public house in Knoeringue all the time? He seems to be a proper alcoholic."

"Please excuse me," said Hunkeler and performed a slight bow. "I hope you have an enjoyable evening." He went back to the table by the entrance and sat down opposite Hedwig. It took him a while to calm down. He hated being railroaded like this. But that's what Basel people were like – extremely reserved in their own city, but encounter them in Alsace and they were all over you, as if you were their best friend.

They ordered the set menu, a bottle of Pommard and mineral water.

"What did the doctor say?" Hedwig asked.

"Nothing specific. He reckons it's possible for someone to experience cognitive disturbances after taking that kind of drug. But I got the impression he didn't think it was likely."

"If it wasn't a dream or a hallucination, then what was it?"

Hunkeler looked at her helplessly. He didn't know.

"Be careful you don't get dragged back into it all. Come on, let's try this wine. And don't look so crabby."

They raised their glasses and drank.

"What exactly does crabby mean, anyway?" he asked.

"Take a look in the mirror, then you'll know."

Hedwig started on her soup, pondering, then evidently decided to try and cheer him up. "What have you been doing all day?" she asked.

"I've been reading."

"Reading what?"

"A book about the First World War."

She put down her spoon. "Oh my God, why? No wonder you look so down. Anyway, who's that guy back there in the corner?"

"Someone I know from the old days. He now has a house in Knoeringue."

Hedwig briefly looked across to Meierhans, a bit put out, then she said: "OK, tell me about your book."

"The best-known book about the First World War is called *Storm of Steel* and is by Ernst Jünger. Jünger was proud of himself for having fought so excellently and for having survived."

"Tales of male heroism," she said. "Yuck."

"There was a farmer from round here who also fought and survived. He wasn't a writer, but he gave a detailed account of what it was like. Nobody knows about his book. And Jünger, that obnoxious, conceited poser, actually rode into Paris on a white horse in the Second World War. I've seen a photo of it."

"Sounds kind of cool, riding up the Champs-Élysées on a white horse," commented Hedwig.

Madame Chappuis brought the roast and topped up their glasses. The wine was exquisite.

"I've been thinking a lot about the past recently," said Hunkeler. "I'm floating in my memories. Do you want to hear about them?"

"OK, go on then."

"When I was twenty I inherited a bit of money from an uncle. It wasn't much, but it was enough to go to Paris for six months. I took the Metro to Place Saint-Michel. That's where I wanted to go, to the Quartier Latin. I was looking for a cheap room, but I had no idea how to go about it. I walked into a house, just some house I liked the look of. I went up the stairs and along a corridor. There was a strange, unfamiliar smell, of ginger perhaps, or cinnamon. I can remember it very clearly, I can still see that hallway in front of me. I didn't come across a single soul. Until a door opened at the back and a girl came out. She was from Thailand or Vietnam. She stopped and looked at me. Her beauty nearly knocked me flat. Then she walked past me to the stairs and smiled at me. Neither of us said a word.

"When I was back out on the street I realized something had happened to me. It was like I was in a trance. I carried on walking until I reached the Carrefour de Buci. That was the right place for me, I felt certain. I went into the Hotel de Dieppe. The house is still there, but it's not a hotel any more. I found the owner on the first floor. He showed me a room in the attic. 'When the weather is bad,' he told me, 'you get some rain coming in here and there. But the corner where the bed is always stays dry.'

"I lived in that room for half a year. It was a wonderful time. I read Verlaine and Apollinaire and wandered about in the streets for hours on end.

"There was a man on the Carrefour de Buci, he had a small monkey on a chain that sat on his shoulder. In front of him stood an old washtub full of potatoes. The potatoes were very cheap. Every morning I bought two pints of milk and drank it straight from the bottle. In the evening I sat in some cafe or another with a glass of red wine."

"Why are you telling me this now?"

"Because it's so vivid in my mind."

"And the Thai girl that smelled of ginger and cinnamon? Did you see her again?" This came somewhat snippily, but Hunkeler ignored it.

"A little later I got together with a girl, we hitchhiked to the coast, to Dunkirk. We spent the night in a hotel room. It was the first time I'd been with a girl all night. In the morning we walked along the sandy beach. The tide was out, the sand was full of seashells and the air was full of salt."

"And your wife, did you meet her in Paris too?"

He realized he'd hurt her feelings. "No. But that's another story. Surely you're not jealous, are you?"

"Me? What gives you that idea? Of course not."

"I just wanted to tell you about all the things that have been going through my head over the past few days. How confident and single-minded I was back then. And how little money I needed. The money is distributed wrongly. These days I could afford to do almost anything, but I no longer have the stamina for it. The money should be given to the young."

He was about to pour the rest of the wine when he was struck by a blow on the shoulder. It was Meierhans, he'd come to their table. "Hunkeler, you old rotter," he bellowed. "Congratulations on your wedding anniversary. Let me get you a schnapps. What do you fancy? Armagnac, cognac, Marc de Bourgogne?"

"Thank you, perhaps another time," Hunkeler replied. "But don't whack me on the shoulder again."

"Please excuse him," said the fiancée. "He's had a bit too much to drink."

"I've earned it," said Meierhans. "Do you remember the old days, Inspector? How we wanted to change the world, all of us in LIST? That was great, we were hardcore. You were in LIST too, weren't you?"

"No. I was just a sympathizer."

"I see, a coward? Shame on you, you sissy. Every proper student was in LIST back then."

"Come on," the woman intervened. "Time to go home to bed." She took Meierhans by the arm and led him out the door.

On Saturday morning, 29 March, Hunkeler drove back to Basel. He'd slept wonderfully in Hedwig's arms and was enjoying the drive. As he reached Trois Maisons the city came into view, glimmering in the sunlight down on the plain. He saw the pharmaceutical company's office tower, which soared more than five hundred feet into the sky. On the right the dark mountains of the Jura stretched along the horizon, and straight ahead the hills of the Black Forest rose in waves, petering out towards the north-west. The snow-covered crest of the Belchen could just be made out.

In Basel he parked outside the house where his apartment was. He walked along to Burgfelderplatz, bought newspapers from the kiosk and entered his neighbourhood bar, the Sommereck.

Edi, the landlord, was sitting at the regulars' table as always. He was alone. In front of him stood a glass containing a grey broth-like mixture that was supposed to help him lose weight. He'd been trying for years, but he still weighed well over two hundred pounds. "Finally, a familiar face," he said. "What can I get you?"

"A white coffee, as usual, and an ashtray. And no griping please," Hunkeler replied.

He lit a cigarette and started leafing through the papers. Edi brought what he'd asked for.

"You know you're not allowed to smoke in here."

Hunkeler nodded and tapped off the ash.

"I don't really mind," Edi continued. "But if the police turn up I'll get a fine. The way they act, you'd think they were driving out the Devil himself."

"I'm only going to smoke the one," said Hunkeler as he reached for the Zurich tabloid. "It's what I do when I read the papers."

Edi mournfully looked at his glass. "Just look at this swill. Terrible. Why shouldn't I eat, if you're smoking? By the way,

I've got some delicious pork sausages from the Black Forest. Fancy some?"

"No thank you. I ate too much yesterday evening."

"Where? And what?"

"In Alsace. Roast veal with morel mushrooms."

"How was it? Juicy and tender?"

Hunkeler nodded.

"Wonderful," enthused Edi. "But don't let me disturb you."

There wasn't a single word about Debrunner in the tabloid.

"It's surprising, don't you think?" said Edi.

"What?"

"That we don't hear anything about Debrunner. I mean, I don't see eye to eye with him politically. I've heard he was a Marxist in his younger years. He's one of those who always comes out ahead, whatever the current trend happens to be. But you've got to give it to him, he's a shrewd politician. Or what do you think?"

Hunkeler thought nothing. He didn't reply.

"Terrible, this red–green majority in Basel," Edi prattled on. "The Germans did away with the GDR twenty-five years ago. Now the GDR is being resurrected right here in Basel. The state dictates and the citizens have to pay up. They've told me I need to renovate the kitchen and the ventilation system. Where am I supposed to get that kind of money from if nobody comes here? Are you sure you don't want to eat anything?"

"Yes."

Edi went behind the counter and fetched a jar of pickled gherkins. He unscrewed the lid and shoved three into his mouth. "Who could have attacked him?" he asked.

Hunkeler shrugged.

"A leading politician is beaten up a few yards from his front door in the Bruderholz district," Edi commented in between chews. "Nobody knows if he's going to survive. And what is Basel doing about it? Absolutely nothing. It stinks to high heaven, if you ask me."

"These days there are people who'll knock someone down simply because they feel like it," Hunkeler told him. "Finding such a perpetrator is almost impossible."

"And you reckon that's what happened?"

"I don't reckon anything at all. It's none of my business any more."

It was unbelievable, the speed at which Edi was devouring the gherkins.

"Surely you're not going to eat the whole jar?" Hunkeler asked.

"Why not? I need some grub in my belly."

"OK then, bring out the sausages. And bread and a glass of white wine. Then we'll eat together like two civilized Christians."


Back at home in his apartment Hunkeler shoved the junk mail into the wastepaper basket, sat down on the balcony and looked out into the back courtyard, which stood bare before him. Someone had chopped down the mighty maple that had spread its branches here. Someone from the city's parks and gardens department, who hadn't deemed it necessary to ask the residents. Now the balconies of the house opposite seemed close enough to touch. On summer evenings, when the heat drove people out onto their balconies, there would be no cooling, voice-dampening foliage any more. People could look straight into each other's bedrooms now, and they could hear everything that was said.

He sat and pondered for a long time. Then he rang directory enquiries and asked for the address and phone number of Lydia Siegenthaler. She lived at 7 Andreasplatz. He dialled the number and heard a high, bright voice. He briefly introduced herself. Of course she remembered him, she said. And yes, she'd be happy to meet with him. Tomorrow at eleven at the Hasenburg.

When he walked across Petersplatz the following morning, the spring sun was glinting through the leafless branches of the elms. He crossed Petersgraben and turned towards the old town. There were no cars about, no pedestrians, it seemed everyone was still asleep in their beds. He descended the steps of the Imbergässlein, named after the holy Imber. This was where Basel was at its most mysterious. Old walls to the left and right, lightless, treeless, a centuries-old fossil, now partly renovated and developed into luxury apartments. It was considered chic to live in the old town.

Down on Schneidergasse he sat down in the sunshine in front of the Hasenburg and ordered coffee and a croissant. He fetched two Sunday newspapers from inside. One of them, a Zurich paper, featured a longish article about Basel, entitled JUNGLE LAW ON THE RHINE? Centred around Debrunner's case, it posed the question whether Basel was still a safe city. Was the feel-good oasis financed by the pharmaceutical industry getting it right? Weren't the red–green do-good idealists going too far in handling the antisocial, parasitic elements, the disability claimants and druggies of every hue with kid gloves? Where would it lead when even esteemed politicians had to fear for their lives in a respectable neighbourhood such as Bruderholz? Answer: To the downfall of law and order, to jungle law.

This report didn't surprise Hunkeler. It was a popular pastime among the Zurich papers to bad-mouth Basel at every opportunity. And Basel didn't have the journalistic means to defend itself against such hostilities. The reach of Basel's local paper was very limited. The city didn't have its own Sunday paper. And the big editorial departments of the national papers were largely based in Zurich.

But perhaps Basel didn't want to defend itself. The people of Basel didn't care what was written about them in Zurich. They were content within their own four walls. They were self-sufficient.

Lydia Siegenthaler arrived at half past eleven. A petite, graceful figure, dark brown eyes, a small diamond ring on her finger. She was wearing a green headscarf. Her voice sounded strangely high-pitched when she greeted him. He wondered why this came as a surprise to him. She hadn't uttered a single word during the nights in the hospital.

"Do you always wear a headscarf?" he asked her.

She smiled at him. "No. Only when I go out. But then always. Why?"

"Because it's unusual these days. Yet I've seen three young women with headscarves recently. Or perhaps four, I'm not too sure any more."

"I come from a rural village," she said. "My grandmother always wore a headscarf when she went to work in the fields.

And anyway, I think it's a really stupid question. Everyone should walk around however they want."

He nodded, he felt ashamed.

"I live in a shared house with several other women, all medical students. We all wear a headscarf when we go out, partly as an act of solidarity with Muslim women."

He lit a cigarette.

"You shouldn't do that."

Hunkeler took two drags and then stubbed the cigarette out. "I rang you up because I wanted to thank you personally," he said. "You were like a guardian angel to me during the nights in the hospital."

"I was just doing my job."

"For me it was more. When you're lying in an unfamiliar bed next to a dying man and hear a church clock strike in the middle of the night, bleak thoughts enter your mind. In those moments it felt like a miracle of resurrection when the door opened and a young, attractive woman walked in with a pill that sent me off into a sweet sleep."

She sniffed at that, a little derisively. She was on her guard now.

"Do you always express yourself so poetically? I thought you were a police officer."

"I was once, but I'm talking to you as a private individual."

She took a gulp of the Campari soda she'd ordered. Her hand was shaking slightly.

"I always dished out a fairly high dose to you. I want the patients to sleep at night."

"And the guy next to me, Fankhauser, did you dish out a high dose to him too?"

Now the smile was gone. She looked at him with a cool, measured gaze.

"Are you even allowed to do this? Interrogate me as though I was in for questioning? I've already had a guy come to see me, an Inspector Madörin, but he showed me his badge."

"I'm not allowed to in any official capacity. But as a private citizen I can. You don't need to answer. You can leave if you want."

But she stayed.

"Dr Fankhauser insisted on remaining conscious during the final days and hours," she said.

"What did he actually die of?"

"Heart failure. Didn't you know that?"

"Yes, that was what I heard."

"At midnight, when I brought you the pill, he was still muttering to himself."

"Was it really midnight? Wasn't it later than that?"

She looked a little taken aback, then she shook her head indignantly.

"Well, it was in the middle of the night, anyway. When I did my final round early in the morning he was dead. And then everything ran its usual course."

"Were you at the funeral in the Minster?"

"No, of course not. Lots of people die in hospital, I can't go to every funeral. Is there anything else you want to ask?"

"Yes. I saw something that night, something that's been preying on my mind. I'm wondering if it was a dream or a hallucination. Or if it really happened."

She waited, wordlessly.

"My doctor thinks it could have been a hallucination, caused by the sleeping pill you gave me. But I don't think so."

"What did you see?"

"I saw a young woman come in. She gave me the pill and waited for me to fall asleep. But I didn't drop off as quickly as she probably thought. I was still awake enough to see her walk over to the other bed and give Fankhauser an injection. Then I fell asleep."

"And who do you think that was? Are you saying that was me? Of course I didn't give Fankhauser an injection, not in the middle of the night."

"I don't know."

"Didn't you recognize the woman's voice?"

"She didn't say a word."

She shook her head, then she eyed him sternly. "Now listen, that's nonsense. You must have been delirious from the pill."

"Maybe someone wanted to release him from his suffering."

Now she smiled again.

"It's possible, isn't it?" he persisted. "Perhaps with an insulin overdose? Which would be very difficult to prove, by the way."

She shook her head again. "That kind of thing doesn't happen in hospital. If someone has to die, then we help them do this in as dignified a manner as possible. But we don't kill them. Why don't you just leave Herr Fankhauser to rest in peace?"

"You think so? Perhaps I should."

"His ashes have been interred. Whatever it was you experienced that night, dream or hallucination, forget about it. Be glad you're back on your feet again."

She drained her glass and stood up.

"It's a beautiful spring day, isn't it? And thank you for the drink."

He stayed sitting there a little while longer and watched as the street filled with people. The first tourists appeared, open guidebooks in their hands. Traders emerged from the nearby market square, where they'd been selling flowers, bread and vegetables. A few winos appeared too, roughly Hunkeler's age; he recognized them from years gone by. They looked at him uncertainly as they walked past and entered the inn without greeting.

Hunkeler decided to drive to Riehen and go for a walk up in Bettingen. As he drove across the Rhine bridge he glanced over to the right, at the facades of Augustinergasse, the old university and the sheer wall of the Pfalz terrace that rose steeply from the river. Behind it, the sandstone of Basel Minster glowed red in the sunshine. Unbelievable, how beautiful Basel could be on a Sunday afternoon.

He crossed Kleinbasel and came to the open stretch of road that offered a clear view of Tüllinger Hill beyond the German border. Up there, in Ötlingen, they produced one of his favourite wines. He decided to stop off at an inn before his walk.

Riehen looked tidy and smart, as if dressed in its Sunday best. It always looked like this, even on weekdays. In centuries past, Riehen was where Basel's aristocrats erected their country estates. Their manor houses were still standing. Like the one of Basel mayor Johann Wettstein, who, following the Thirty Years War, had secured independence for the Swiss Confederation in the Peace of Westphalia treaties. He was a significant historic figure, as Hunkeler had been told at school. What Hunkeler hadn't been told was that this Wettstein had ordered the beheading of Basel's peasant leaders during the Peasants' War of 1653. That he had found out for himself.

He turned off right, towards Bettingen, and drove through a gently upward-sloping villa district. A balmy spring breeze wafted in through the open window. There was a noticeable absence of cars parked on the street. They were all tucked away in private garages to protect them from rain and hail.

Both Riehen and Bettingen were in the section of Basel City territory that lay on the right bank of the Rhine. A beautiful, quiet setting, good air, and a high level of achievement even among the younger school pupils. You could go for wonderful hikes from here, across the German border to Grenzach-am-Rhein or through the forest to Inzlingen.

Hunkeler pulled up outside the country inn, went inside and sat down at a table where an old woman was eating soup. Smartly turned out in a freshly ironed, pale blue blouse and golden earrings, she sat bolt upright in her chair. Going by the delicious smell in the room, the soup she was eating was probably a meat broth.

"The same as this lady here, please, and a glass of red Ötlinger," said Hunkeler.

Only half the tables were occupied. At one of them the landlord, dressed in a white chef's jacket, was sharing a half-bottle of white with two men. There was a family with three children, tired from their hike, some day trippers, and three old women playing a card game in the corner at the back. An almost festive serenity and stillness prevailed in the room, interrupted only by the occasional chiming of a wall clock.

"Is it tasty?" Hunkeler asked the woman at his table as she carefully chewed on a piece of meat.

She nodded. "The meat is good. If only the teeth were better. Why do you ask?"

"Oh, sorry," he said. "I didn't mean to disturb you. Please forgive me."

"You're not disturbing me. I like chatting to people. I used to talk a lot as part of my work, you see."

Her name was Martina Ehringer. She had once been a schoolteacher in Riehen.

"In that case you must have known Stephan Fankhauser," said Hunkeler. "I was at university with him."

"Yes, Steffi, of course I knew him, I was his teacher. I went to the funeral in the Minster. He went far in life. He became quite an important figure, despite everything."

Hunkeler spread some horseradish sauce onto a piece of meat and popped it in his mouth. "I heard at the funeral that his father was a border guard," he said.

"Yes, that's correct. Old Joseph Fankhauser. He worked on the border crossing to Lörrach-Stetten. He was a very strict man. Did you say you were a friend of Steffi's?"

"We were at university together."

"Oh, were you? Nobody would have thought university was on the cards for Steffi. He did get good marks right from the outset. But he was very introverted, inhibited somehow. His father was brutally oppressive, you see. He would completely pull him to pieces. And he beat Steffi whenever it pleased him. That's just what he was like, old Fankhauser. He was from the Emmental, from somewhere near Langnau, I think. Firm but fair, as they used to call it. And deferential to the authorities to the point of self-abandonment. That's why

Steffi went so overboard later with the revolutionary stuff. He was a real communist as a young adult. Old Fankhauser felt deeply ashamed about it."

She pushed her plate away. It still contained a large piece of meat.

"I turned eighty last November. I don't eat much these days. It's not meat I live off any more, I live off my memories."

She smiled at him amiably.

"It's very nice that you're taking the time to talk to me. One does grow lonely as the years pass. And I'm an old spinster, Monsieur."

He smiled back at her. "And Steffi's mother, what was she like?" he asked.

"Marietta? She was friendly and full of life. And intelligent. I never understood why the two of them got together. I think she suffered, being married to him. She died quite young. Well, they were hard times back then, for all of us. Riehen and Bettingen wouldn't have been defended in the Second World War if the Wehrmacht had decided to march in. We were sitting ducks, so to speak. And almost every day refugees came over the border, pitiful figures. Many had to be sent back. Those were the orders. Marietta couldn't bear it. It broke her heart."

She dabbed the corners of her mouth with her napkin, then she looked at him with her old, sad eyes.

"There were many who couldn't bear it. But that's what it was like back then. Why does it interest you?"

"I was sharing the hospital room with Steffi when he died."

"Oh, were you? Well, despite everything, he had a very successful career, didn't he? It was really nice to chat to you, Monsieur."

She stood up laboriously and reached for the walking stick leaning against the wall.

"By the way, I've collected quite a few things from those times. If you're interested, you can call me. My number is in the phone book."

He watched her as she carefully hobbled out.

The following week, Hunkeler decided to saw up the spruce that had been snapped in half by a November storm. The upper part had been torn away by the wind and hurled to the ground, narrowly missing the barn roof. On Hunkeler's request, a neighbour with a tractor had come and pulled out the lower part with the roots. It would be good firewood, good kindling.

He fetched the chainsaw from the barn and was about to start it up when he heard a buzzing. It was coming from the willow tree, which was in full bloom. It was a monotonous, insistent, incredible hum that gained an almost deafening intensity when Hunkeler walked over and sat down on the bench by the willow's trunk. It was the music of the bees. The whole tree was buzzing, the whole garden, the world.

He listened, with growing rapture. The mysterious thing about this music was that it remained constant and unchanging, poised on a single note. No rising or falling, no pianissimo, no crescendo, it always remained the same. And perhaps that was what made it so beguiling.

Every spring it amazed him anew. That they were back again, resurrected after their long winter sleep, heading straight for the first flowering willow. Thinking this made him feel almost devout.

He knew that François, who lived further along by the stream, was a beekeeper. Perhaps he should ask him sometime how it was done. He had plenty of time, and space for more willows. And there were lots of plum, cherry, apple and pear trees round here. They flowered too and were visited by the bees. No doubt there were also other bee-friendly shrubs and trees that he could plant to invite the bees for more happy buzzing.

Hunkeler realized that, actually, he still had a nice life ahead of him. If you can ponder whether or not to take up beekeeping in your later years, you're doing pretty well, he thought. There was no reason to feel depressed in any way. And no reason to be puzzling over mysterious night nurses that smelled of nutmeg or some such thing.

Sitting there, under the willow tree, he felt content with his life. And he decided to finally get on with the work and tackle the spruce trunk.

Just then someone appeared out on the street. A girl, a young woman. She was carrying a travel bag and had a yellow headscarf wrapped around her hair. She seemed to be looking for something.

He'd never seen her before. But the way she walked, the manner in which she held her head as she stopped and looked across to him, made him realize it was Estelle, his granddaughter.

He stood up and slowly walked towards her. "Are you Estelle?" he asked.

"Yes. If you're my *grand-père*."

They looked at each other. He didn't know what else to say.

"*Tu es mon grand-père?*"

"I think so, yes. Where on earth have you come from? I mean, how did you get here?"

"I hitchhiked. He took all of my things. Even *le mobile*, so I wouldn't be able to call anyone."

"Who?"

"*Mon père*, the bastard. I have no money, nothing. He wanted to lock me up."

"Is he that bad?"

She nodded. She put the bag down and for a moment she seemed close to falling over.

"*Oui*. Because I'm pregnant. But I'm eighteen, I'm an adult. Can I stay here?"

She looked fragile, and exhausted. Hunkeler picked up the bag.

"Come in. I'll make us a cup of tea. Are you hungry?"

She nodded. They went into the kitchen. He put water on to boil for the tea and fished out what he had. Bread, cheese, liver pâté, pickled gherkins.

"Do you like fried eggs?"

"*Oui, grand-père.*"

She seemed famished, she tucked in with gusto.

"So you just ran away from home?" he asked. "And they don't know where you are?"

"*Non. Maman* knows. She suggested I should come and stay with you."

"How long have you been on the road?"

"Since yesterday. I didn't tell my father anything. Perhaps he knows from *maman. Il est trop con.* He's such a dick. He's Moroccan."

She took off her headscarf, folded it up and placed it in the bag.

"He wants me to wear a headscarf when I go out. So paternalistic. *Dégueulasse.* It's disgusting."

He cut another slice of bread for her and spread butter on it.

"And your boyfriend?"

"What boyfriend?"

"The father of your child."

"Oh, that. I only said that so you would invite me in. You're not going to chuck me out now, are you, *grand-père*?"

"Do you mean you're not actually pregnant at all?"

"*Mais non.* I'm not pregnant." She smiled at him. She obviously felt confident now.

"That's a dirty trick, lying to me like that. I was really worried."

"Worried? Why?"

"OK. Perhaps also a bit excited."

She had polished off the liver pâté and was eating the last piece of bread.

"Sometimes you have to lie to get what you're after, *n'est-ce pas*? Don't you think, *grand-père*?"

"Yes, perhaps."

"I'm tired now. Where can I sleep?"

"In the little guest room above Hedwig's room."

"Hedwig is nice, *très sympa*. Do you love her?"

Hunkeler sat there like a schoolboy who didn't know the answer. Then he nodded.

"Right, come on. I'll show you your bed."

He led her up to the guest room and set the bag down on the table. Estelle gazed bemused at the old bedstead with its ornate woodwork.

"*Comme un bateau*, like a boat. In a bed like that, nothing can happen to you, *n'est-ce pas, grand-père*?"

She stepped out of her shoes and slipped under the red and white checked duvet. "*Je reste ici*," she said. "I'm staying put."

"Do you want a nightgown?"

"Nightgown? What's that?"

"*Une chemise de nuit.* Or some pyjamas?"

She laughed. She probably found him droll.

"Yes please. *Une chemise de nuit, s'il te plaît.*"

Hedwig came in the evening. Hunkeler was in the kitchen, grating potatoes for a rösti.

"And?" she quizzed him.

"And what?"

"Are the two of you getting along?"

"Well, I'm getting along with her. And I suspect she finds me quite *sympa*."

He set the frying pan on the stove and scattered the bacon lardons in it. When the fat started to melt he added the potatoes. He seasoned and stirred. Then he set the flame to low.

"Are you angry with me?" she asked.

"Not really. But how is this all going to work?"

Hedwig poured herself a cup of tea. "I think it's about time you did something for your family," she commented.

"Excuse me, who left whom? Did I leave my wife, or did she leave me?"

"That's really not Estelle's fault."

"What's up with her dad, anyway? Do you know anything about him?"

"I've met him a few times. He seems nice."

"Why am I never told anything?" he shouted. "What am I? Some kind of dimwit?"

"Shush, you'll wake her up."

"She just comes wandering in like a stray cat and curls up in the bed. *Oui, grand-père, n'est-ce pas, grand-père.* And her father is Moroccan and wants her to wear a headscarf. I'm taking her back, first thing tomorrow."

Hedwig burst out laughing. She was shaking with laughter.

"It's not funny!" he shouted.

But then he had to laugh too. He fetched a sheet of paper and put it on the table.

"Where does she live?"

"In Les Prés. It's a hamlet in the Vosges mountains, near Thann. Her father has a junkyard, old cars mainly. He sells spare parts that are no longer available commercially. He also sells music boxes and all sorts of knick-knacks. He sometimes comes to the flea market on Petersplatz."

"Write everything down. Exact address and phone numbers, his and Isabelle's. I'm going to have words with the guy."

Hedwig wrote everything down on the piece of paper as requested.

"You should switch off the gas, otherwise we'll end up with a burned rösti."

He turned off the flame, tipped the rösti onto a plate and put it on the table. It had a beautiful golden crust.

"She's an adult," said Hedwig. "She's French, but she also has Swiss citizenship, so she can work in Basel. She can live with me until she's found her own place."

"I see you've got it all worked out already. And what do you want me to do?"

"You can look after her for a bit. And find her a job."

"Oh yes? And where? And how?"

She had to laugh again. "Be happy, *grand-père.*"

Estelle wanted to have *un mobile*, right now, *absolument tout de suite*. So they drove to Altkirch to buy one.

"Where did you sleep?" Hunkeler asked her as they cruised through Hundsbach.

"When?"

"That night when you were travelling."

"In Mulhouse."

"But I thought you didn't have any money."

"I had a little bit. I sat myself in a bar by the station, where the young people go. I knew two of them, they helped me. *Pourquoi?* Why do you want to know?"

"A young woman like you. I mean, isn't that dangerous?"

She smiled at him with bright eyes. "That's so sweet. *Tu es gentil, grand-père.*"

"So what have you been up to until now? Have you been at school? Or in an apprenticeship?"

"I've been at school and I've worked a little. Bar work, at the Sauterelle in Thann. It's a kind of disco. *Sauterelle* means grasshopper."

"I know. *Heugümper*, we call them in Swiss."

"Every summer, *je suis partie*. I escaped. *Dans le midi*, down to the Mediterranean. You go nuts if you stay in the Vosges. People say the Vosges mountains are wonderful for hiking. But nobody comes hiking. Occasionally you see a wrinkled old couple that can barely stay on their feet. That's why I ran away."

89

"And what do you want to become?"

"Become? Why? Time passes whether I become anything or not."

In Tagsdorf Hunkeler nearly didn't spot the speed bump they'd installed across the road to curb the speeding. He slammed his foot on the brakes. "*Merde, les cochons!*" he cursed.

She laughed out loud as the car jolted. "You swear in French, *grand-père*?"

"*Mais bien sûr.* Of course. I lived in Paris for a while."

They turned onto the main road that connected Mulhouse with Altkirch. Trucks with trailers were clogging up the road and the heavy traffic slowed to a crawl.

"And Isabelle?" he asked. "Do you get on with her?"

"Maman? *Elle est un peu bizarre,* she's a bit odd. But kind of OK for her age. She's nice to me. She has her goats. They keep her happy."

"Goats? How many does she have?"

"A dozen. Perhaps more. She makes cheese, or at least she tries to. *Du chèvre,* terrible. She even sells it."

She wrinkled her nose and shook her short hair.

"Do I look like *maman*?"

He nodded. "I recognized you the minute I saw you. The way you stood there, your posture and everything."

"Oh yuck, *dégueulasse.*"

"Not at all. I think it's nice that you look like Isabelle."

"And *grand-maman*, do I look like her too?"

The traffic had ground to a halt. Hunkeler switched off the engine. He felt her gaze resting on him, bright, inquisitive. But he didn't reply.

"Tell me about Paris," she requested.

"What shall I tell you? It's all a very long time ago."

"How old were you?"

"Two years older than you."

"And what did you do there all day, and at night?"

He thought for a long time.

"Near where I was staying, there was a bistro that was open around the clock. It was called Le Bouquet and was down a side alley off the Boulevard Saint-Germain. It was nothing special, just an ordinary, typical bistro, like countless others back then. It had a bar, where people would stand for a short while to drink a coffee. Along the wall were a few tables, which were usually empty. I often went there around midnight, to end the day with a beer."

"Alone?"

"Yes, alone."

"*Pourquoi?* Why alone?"

"I don't know. Because I wanted to be alone. One night I was sitting at one of those little tables when a girl came in. She briefly looked at me and then came and sat down. She ordered coffee, I remember that. She was from Germany. She said she'd arranged to meet someone at six in the morning in a cafe by the Jardin du Luxembourg. We sat there together until shortly before six. We talked, cautiously, inquisitively. We watched the customers as they came and went. We watched as dawn broke. Delivery vans arrived, a baker with a basket full of bread. Sleepy faces. The first *cafés au lait* were ordered, and sandwiches with ham or cheese. Then we walked to the cafe where she was going to meet her friend. I can still remember hearing the blackbirds sing in the Jardin du Luxembourg. It struck me as strange in the middle of the city. We briefly said goodbye, I didn't turn round as I walked away. On the way back I realized I didn't know her name. And she didn't know mine."

"And you never saw her again?"

"No."

"What did she look like?"

"Well, she just looked like girls look. Beautiful."

Estelle thought for a while. Then she nodded. "I want to go there too," she said.


When they drove back two hours later, there were three of them in the car. Hunkeler at the wheel, Estelle on the back seat, clamping the phone to her ear with one hand, the other holding onto the collar of a goat they had stowed in the boot.

Estelle was talking very fast into the phone, in French, and Hunkeler couldn't catch everything she was saying. But he understood enough to know she was telling her girlfriend how she had gone to the market in Altkirch with her *grand-père* and bought a goat. Yes, yes, he's nice, *très sympa. Un peu drôle*, kind of funny, but cute, *oui, mignon*. He has beds that look like boats you could sail out to sea on. *Mais oui*, she was fine, she was going to stay here for a while.

She shoved her phone into her pocket. "I will call her Lucie," she announced. "Jacqueline would be nice too, but Lucie is more elegant. What do you think, *grand-père?*"

He nodded briefly and muttered something to himself.

"Are you angry?"

"No, annoyed."

"Never mind. Lucie will cheer you up. Goats are great to talk to, they can laugh. Did you know that, *grand-père?*"

"Yes, dammit. She's probably laughing her head off already."

"Don't be silly, *grand-père*."

"Will you quit calling me *grand-père* all the time!" he barked. "My name is Peter, not *grand-père*."

She was offended now, she put on a sulky face.

"Sorry, I didn't mean to get cross at you," he said. "But who's going to look after her?"

"Me, of course. I know how to look after goats."

"And when you're not here?"

"You. You've got plenty of time after all. She's still young, she doesn't need to be milked. We just need to give her milk. We can get that from your neighbour. You'll see, it'll be fine."

Hunkeler turned off into the Hundsbach valley and drove slowly through the villages, in second gear. Perhaps she was right, he thought while she was chatting on the phone again. Perhaps it would work. He had plenty of space, and straw in the barn. There was still a load of old hay up in the hayloft too. And if things got difficult he could take the goat over to the neighbour.

He carried on grumbling to himself nevertheless. He had simply been caught off guard by this minx of a granddaughter. By her speedy decision. It had all happened so fast, he'd never got a chance to object.

"Go and tie her to the walnut tree," he said as he switched off the engine outside his house. "I'll get a pen ready for her. Will she eat hay?"

"She will if she doesn't get anything else. But she'd much rather have fresh grass."

"Well, she's a bit ahead of things on that. The grass has to grow first."

"Diluted cow's milk, she likes that. Do you have a baby bottle?"

"Why? Surely she can drink from a bucket."

Hunkeler went into the barn, pulled down two bales of straw and scattered them across the old calf pen. Then he fetched hay. Let's see if this is good enough for Madame Lucie, he thought. If not, then to hell with her.

But then he had to grin despite himself. A goat, not such a bad idea. He could hear her scraping at the ground, bucking, bleating. He felt like an old farmer, a kind of Robinson who'd taken in a stray animal. And perhaps there would be offspring one day.

He heard Estelle come in. She was white as a ghost, and shaking. "The lock on the front door has been bashed in," she said. "There's someone in the house. A man."

"What? Did you see him?"

"Yes, through the glass in the kitchen door. *Est-ce qu'il est méchant?* Is he dangerous?"

"No, of course not. You don't need to be scared."

But her shaking unsettled him. He could feel the hairs on the back of his neck stand up. In the middle of the day, ridiculous. He went over to the chopping block and picked up the small axe. Then he walked out onto the forecourt and quietly approached the door. Yes, someone had given the old lock a good kick and burst it open.

He briefly considered his next move, then went back into the barn, put the axe away again and fetched a bundle of rags down from a beam. It contained the old handgun he had inherited from his father. The gun was loaded, but he didn't know whether the cartridges would still ignite. He removed the clip and transferred the ammunition to his left jacket pocket. Then he slotted the clip back in and placed the gun in his right pocket.

"Are you going to shoot, *grand-père*?" asked Estelle, who had followed him.

"Of course not. I just feel safer with a gun. You stay here and don't move."

She nodded, trembling with excitement.

He quietly crossed the forecourt, stepped inside the house and pushed open the kitchen door. He saw Christian Moor sitting at the table, in front of him a glass and a half-empty bottle of wine.

"Oh, it's you," said Hunkeler. "What are you doing here?"

"You have to help me," Moor replied.

"Have you gone mad? Why did you kick in my front door? Now the lock is broken. That's no way to enter a neighbour's house."

Moor was white as a sheet, apart from the red blotches on his cheeks that probably stemmed from the wine.

"What's the matter?" Hunkeler asked.

"I'm not going back to the hospital. No way. And I'm not going to prison either."

Prison? This startled Hunkeler.

"What have you done?"

Moor's hands started to shake violently. He wrapped them around the wine glass to calm himself down, but the shaking didn't stop.

"Nothing. It wasn't me. I swear to God."

Hunkeler fetched a glass, poured himself some wine and took a big gulp.

"So what the hell's happened?"

"Philipp Meierhans was shot this morning. By the edge of the forest, near the big oak where he waits to ambush wild boar. Shot dead with his own rifle. I walked past there at nine this morning. I go for the same walk every day. Now they think I've killed him."

"And? Did you kill him? Perhaps there was a scuffle, a quarrel? Perhaps a shot got discharged from the rifle by accident."

Moor looked up at him from tormented, watery eyes. A reddish haze covered the whites.

"I could never kill another person. Anyway, I always gave him a wide berth whenever I saw him from a distance."

Hunkeler drained his glass. He took the bottle, shoved the cork back in and put it on the floor.

"So you're a suspect. And you're a wanted person. That means you have to hand yourself in, whether you're guilty or not. I'm going to call Inspector Bardet in Mulhouse. I know him, he's a good man. He will come and pick you up."

Moor grabbed the bread knife that was lying on the table and jumped up. But Hunkeler was faster. He already had the gun in his hand.

"Don't do anything stupid now. What must be, must be. If you're innocent, you'll soon be free again."

Estelle appeared in the door. She stared at Moor, who was standing in the corner.

"Clear off," Hunkeler growled.

Estelle disappeared.

"They'll find you anyway. Meierhans bought your house and threw you out. So you have a strong motive."

"No, please don't," Moor pleaded.

"I have to."

Hunkeler fished out his phone and tried to enter a number with his free hand. He laid the gun on the table. There, that was easier. He saw Moor grab the gun with lightning speed and point it at him. "Don't make me do it. Please," he whined.

"Do what? I thought you couldn't kill anyone."

"I can kill myself," said Moor as he raised the gun to his temple and pulled the trigger. There was a dry clicking sound and Moor crumpled, half leaning against the wall.

"What a mess," said Hunkeler. "Goddammit."

He picked up the gun that had fallen on the ground, then he pulled the old man up and sat him back on the chair. He fetched the bottle and poured.

"Calm down. I just wanted to be sure you really mean it. There, drink."

Moor drank. He was still shaking. Estelle reappeared in the door.

"It's all going to be OK," Hunkeler said to Moor. "This is Estelle; Estelle, this is the artist Christian Moor." He turned to face Estelle. "Take Madame Lucie to her pen and tie her up. And tell her she'll get milk in the evening."

Estelle nodded and disappeared.

"I thought I was going to die," said Moor.

"Now listen to me carefully. I believe you that you're innocent. But I can't have you staying in the house. The gendarmerie will come here soon and ask me whether you're here. I'll tell them that you came in and drank a glass of wine, but that I don't know anything about Meierhans and I don't know where you went. Who knows, perhaps you'll decide to go and hide in the hayloft. Whatever you do, I haven't got a clue. And now get lost."

He watched as Moor stood up and walked out unsteadily. Then Hunkeler fetched some tools and set about repairing the lock. It was easy enough, there was no permanent damage. It was clear that anyone who wanted to come into his house could do so. And that was fine by Hunkeler.

They came around three o'clock, Commissaire François Bardet and two officers Hunkeler didn't know. He was relieved to see they didn't have a dog with them.

"What's going on?" Bardet asked. "Someone is shot, you have the suspect in your house and you don't contact us? Not what I'd expect from a colleague."

"I was a colleague, but I'm not any more," Hunkeler corrected him. "Whatever you do, it's never right. If you get in touch, you're told to stop interfering. If you don't get in touch, it's not right either. Who told you he was here?"

"A man who lives further along, by the stream. He saw him and rang us. It seems that Monsieur Moor was on his way to you. Are you a friend of his?"

"No, just an acquaintance."

"*Quand-même*, he still came here. Where is he now?"

"I don't know."

Bardet fished out a document. "This is an *ordre de perquisition*, a search warrant. *Allez-y*, get to work."

Hunkeler stepped aside to give the two officers access to the stairs. "Go ahead, but he isn't here." He turned to Bardet. "Can I offer you a schnapps?"

"Why not."

They went into the kitchen. Hunkeler retrieved a bottle of old damson schnapps from the bottom of the cupboard.

"My neighbour made it with the damsons from my tree. Cheers."

They downed the schnapps. Bardet lit a cigarette. He clearly felt uncomfortable about the whole business. They liked each other too much.

"Still a chain-smoker?" Hunkeler asked.

"*Merde*, yes. I can't get away from it. And you?"

"Now and then. But there are days when I manage without."

"What do you do all day long?"

"I read a lot. I listen to the bees. I have a goat."

"Hunkeler turns farmer," Bardet laughed.

They heard a clattering from upstairs. The officers must have opened the large wardrobe, the one with the loose hinges on the left door wing.

"It's OK," said Hunkeler. "That door always falls off. It wasn't Moor, by the way." He poured another schnapps for Bardet.

"Thank you," said the Commissaire. "And you?"

"No, one is enough."

Bardet downed the second schnapps. "Tastes fabulous. And yes, that's my opinion too. Still, he's a suspect. We have to question him."

"He was in the Friedmatt psychiatric hospital. He said he's never going back there again. Or into custody. He was a

99

good painter, quite successful. But in recent years he's faded into obscurity. He's not coping with it very well."

"As happens to many artists," commented Bardet. "We're better off in that respect, *n'est-ce pas?*"

Going by the sounds from upstairs, the two officers were in the attic now. There was a loud cursing; one of them must have hit his head.

"I heard Meierhans was shot with his own rifle," said Hunkeler. "Was there a fight?"

Bardet looked out at the garden, where Fritz the cockerel was limbering up to one of his pathetic crows. "*Mon dieu,* still the same old cockerel," he said. "What do the hens say to that?"

They grinned at each other.

"It's possible there was a fight," Bardet continued. "A single shot was fired, which hit his carotid. But we don't know who he fought with. Moor would certainly have a motive."

The officers could be heard coming down the stairs now. They appeared in the kitchen door. "*Rien, chef,*" one of them reported. "Nobody here, *do isch niemer.*"

"*Bon,*" said Bardet. "That was it. The search is over."

They stepped out onto the forecourt.

"Do you really have a goat?"

"Yes," said Hunkeler.

"I like goats. My grandmother had some. Can I see her?"

Hunkeler opened the barn door and they went in. Bardet switched on his flashlight. The light pierced the gloom, illuminating old oil drums, bald tyres, broken wheelbarrows. The beam fell onto the pen in the back corner, revealing the head of a goat peering over the side.

"Well I never," muttered Bardet. "*Une chèvre.*"

The Commissaire went over to her, shining the light into the pen. There was a figure lying in the straw, wrapped in an old wool blanket. The figure appeared to be sleeping.

"And look at that. Who do we have here?" said Bardet. He reached for the hay fork leaning against the wall and gave the sleeping figure several prods in the side. "A visitor, hiding in the goat pen. What do you say to this then, Hunkeler?"

A hand emerged from the blanket, then another, delicate, slim hand. Estelle's short hair appeared, her head, her sleepy face. She sat up. "What's going on, *grand-père*?" she asked. "Why are you waking me up?"

"Sorry, you carry on sleeping," said Hunkeler. "Don't worry about these men." And to Bardet, "This is my granddaughter Estelle. And this is Madame Lucie."

In the evening he took a bucket and went over to his neighbour's cowshed to get milk for the goat. "I have a visitor," he said. "My granddaughter. She's staying with me for a few days."

"I didn't know you had a *petite-fille*. I saw her standing up by the road this morning. I wondered what she was looking for. That's nice, *n'est-ce pas*? *Si jolie*, such a lovely *petite-fille*."

"Yes, but she's very wilful. She was determined to get a young goat."

"I see. And now you need milk for the animal. The wilfulness didn't come from nowhere, by the way. She got that from her *grand-père*."

She smiled at him. A still-handsome woman, it struck him as she stood there in her boots and briefly brushed a strand of grey hair aside. Every morning and every evening she's in here, he thought, year after year, and milks three cows, even though nobody wants to buy the milk from her any more.

"Do you never get bored of the work?" he asked.

"*Mais non, c'est ma vie*. It's my life. What else would I be doing? With animals there's life in the place. Otherwise the shed would stand empty."

She pointed to the bucket.

"But she can't drink out of that. She needs something she can suck from. Wait a moment."

She went round the back to the pigsty and returned with a feeding bucket that had a teat attached.

"And?" she asked. "Have they found him?"

Hunkeler was taken aback. "Who?"

"The man who was here before. The one with the red jacket, Monsieur Moor. In this good weather I'm in the garden all day. *Vous savez*, planting salad and vegetables. I saw him kick open your door."

"No, they haven't found him. I don't even know whether he's still in one of the outbuildings. They weren't interested in doing a thorough search, otherwise they would have had a dog with them."

"But they know he was here?"

"Yes."

"He's probably hiding somewhere in the hayloft. Or what do you think?"

"I don't know. What I do know is that he didn't kill Meierhans. I'm sure of that."

She switched off the milking machine and poured some milk into the bucket.

"You have to thin the milk with water. Otherwise she'll get the runs. I'm not particularly nosy, *nid das Si meine, i sig bsunders curieuse.* But you can't help noticing things, *mir gseht halt alls.* Everyone knows everybody's business in the village. Sometimes that's nice, sometimes not. People are glad when something happens, *wen eppis passiert.* Otherwise it gets boring. *N'est-ce pas?*"

He nodded. He wasn't sure what to say.

"My niece rang me earlier," she continued. "*Ma nièce,* she lives in Knoeringue. She thinks it was the Krotzers' lad. He's against everything. Against the large tractors, against the maize, against hunting. She thinks he tried to take Meierhans' rifle off him and a shot got discharged in the tussle. *Mais si c'est vrai?* My niece doesn't know if it's true."

"Why doesn't she report it to the police?"

"*Non,* she can't do that. *Das goht nid.* Nobody in the village would ever talk to her again."

It was after seven in the evening and Hunkeler was sitting in the kitchen with Estelle, eating the risotto he had cooked. Madame Lucie had drunk the milk, and they both felt pleased. It didn't work too well at first. She refused and kicked up a terrible fuss. She tried to knock over the milk bucket, leaped high into the air and whirled up all the straw in the pen. But then Estelle shoved two fingers into her mouth and Lucie started to suck on them. Relieved, they watched as the goat drank half the bucket.

"Do you think that's enough now, *grand-père?*" Estelle asked.

"No idea. I don't know how much milk a young goat needs."

"Well, I think it's enough now. We'll give her the rest in the morning."

Estelle pulled the bucket away. Lucie tilted her head to one side and gave a short bleat. She seemed to be laughing.

"She's happy now, *grand-père*. And tomorrow we'll go for a walk with her. You'll see, she's going to like being here with us."

"Don't you think she might feel a bit lonely? All by herself, without any other goats?"

"*Mais non.* She's got me. And she's got you."

Her optimism was astounding. And infectious, thought Hunkeler. He stroked the goat's head and tried to ruffle her fur. Apparently she didn't like that. She preferred to nibble on his shirt sleeve. "Stop it, you little beast," he growled. "You're not getting my shirt."

Back in the kitchen, Estelle immediately got on the phone to three of her friends, Claudine, Liliane and Ladina. She rang them one after the other, to report that Lucie had drunk the milk. That was fine by Hunkeler, it meant he could concentrate on the risotto. And on his thoughts.

Why did he like the girl so much? From the very first moment, when he'd seen her standing on the street. Was it down to family bonds? The blood tie between them? Or was it the beauty of her youth? The unquestioning way she simply accepted him as her grandfather? He felt a little spooked by it. What were the consequences for him, who was used to doing exactly as he pleased? Was he responsible for her now? And what other beasts was she going to drag into his house?

He pushed these thoughts aside. In some ways he rather enjoyed having her here. He certainly took great care not to overcook the risotto.

She was on the phone again while they ate. Claudine had called back, apparently there were still some questions that needed answering.

Hunkeler heard the front door being opened, very quietly, and being pulled shut again. He stiffened, fork in hand.

Estelle looked at him in alarm and switched her phone off.

"What is it, *grand-père*? Is it that man?"

He nodded. They both listened, but there were no other sounds.

"Come into the kitchen, Moor," Hunkeler called out. "Come and sit with us and have something to eat. The Commissaire is long gone. He won't be back any time soon."

Estelle leaped up and was about to run for the back door.

"You stay here," Hunkeler told her.

The kitchen door opened and Moor came in. He looked pathetic standing there in his red jacket, covered in strands of hay.

"Will you take that bloody jacket off. It's plenty warm enough in here."

Hunkeler moved a chair round for Moor and dished him up some risotto. Moor's hands were shaking so much he could barely hold the fork. "I need wine," he said. "Urgently. I can't eat anything until I've had wine. I need at least two bottles a day."

Hunkeler fetched some wine and poured him a glass.

"There's plenty of wine. It's here, next to the cupboard. And there's more in the cellar. Cheers."

Moor raised the glass to his lips with both hands and drained it. Hunkeler topped him up.

"Now eat. Take your time. You can sleep here, in the small room next to the bathroom. Tomorrow we'll think about what to do."

Moor put a forkful of rice in his mouth. He chewed for a long time before he swallowed.

"Why are you helping me?"

Hunkeler pretended not to have heard the question. "If anyone from the gendarmerie or from Basel comes, you go out through the back door," he told him. "But not if it's my girlfriend. I've spoken to her on the phone."

"You were a police officer. You should be reporting me."

"True. But I've arrested plenty of people in my life. And anyway, we're in France. I have no authority to arrest you. My neighbour knows you're here, by the way."

Moor wanted to jump to his feet, but Hunkeler held him back.

"Stay where you are. She's not going to say anything. People don't think much of the police round here. But it would be best if you took yourself off somewhere. To Paris for example. Don't you have anyone who can help you?"

"No. And anyway, you know I wouldn't get far. So do you believe me?"

"It's not about whether I believe you," Hunkeler told him. "I've believed many things and been given the run-around. But I can see what a state you're in, the picture of misery."

Moor's hands were less shaky now. He ate with increasing appetite. "This is good," he commented. "Did you cook it?"

Hunkeler nodded. It really did taste good. Estelle now carried on eating too, but she kept a watchful eye on the old man.

"It's the worst thing that can possibly happen to an artist," said Moor. "To survive your own success. I should have died ages ago, long before my wife. But my heart keeps on beating. It beats and beats and forces me to live and to work. Even though nobody gives two hoots about me any more."

Estelle fished out a tissue to give to Moor, but Hunkeler shook his head. Let the guy have a weep, he thought.

"My recent pictures are no worse than the earlier ones. In fact I would say they're better. They're more fundamental, restricted to the essential. But my time was suddenly over, virtually from one day to the next. All of a sudden, nobody wanted to buy my paintings any more. People barely wanted to look at them. They even made fun of me behind my back, I was well aware of that. Oil on canvas, how old-fashioned. Rain in southern Alsace, how trivial, how insignificant. Yet I carried on painting. It's all I knew how to do. I lowered the prices, but it made no difference. I would have happily given my paintings away if someone had taken them, hung them on a wall and looked at them every now and then. Eventually I couldn't bear it any more. I actually intended to burn myself together with my pictures. But when it came to it I didn't have the courage."

"And so for all of this you wanted to take revenge on Meierhans?"

A look of alarm shot across Moor's face. He seemed to have emerged from his anguished memories and was on his guard now.

"What? Why?"

"Perhaps you grabbed him, wrenched the rifle out of his hands and shot him? That could be what happened, couldn't it?"

Moor pulled out a handkerchief and wiped his eyes, his drooping mouth, his stubbly chin. He thought for a while, then he slowly shook his head.

"The truth is that I really was angry at the guy. I shouted at him, told him he was a miserable swine. And I slapped my hand down on his rifle. But he was stronger than me. He aimed the rifle at me and yelled at me to get lost, otherwise he was going to blast my head off. Those were his words. Then I fled into the woods. That's what happened, it's the honest truth."

"Who knows?" Hunkeler opened another bottle and poured himself a glass too. "Perhaps. Perhaps not."

"I can't bear it when people don't believe me," said Moor. "Art is about truth, about the search for it. All my life I have tried to portray the truth. I have endeavoured to always speak the truth. An artist who lies is not an artist, he is a hoaxer. Am I a hoaxer?"

"No, I don't think you're a hoaxer. But you're pretty drunk."

From outside, Hedwig's car could be heard pulling onto the forecourt.

"Don't worry, it's just my girlfriend," said Hunkeler. "Now pull yourself together please."

The door opened and Hedwig came in. "Are you crazy, Peter?" she berated Hunkeler. "Don't you know he's a wanted man?"

"I do. Bardet was here. He cleared off again quite quickly."

"Did you hide him?"

"He hid himself. Bardet also thinks it wasn't Moor. Sit down and join us for a drink. He's going to stay the night."

Moor got up and attempted a bow. "*Bonsoir*, Madame. It's a pleasure."

"Sit down, Herr Moor," Hedwig barked at him. "I like your paintings a lot, but you can't simply turn up here like this. Don't you know Herr Meierhans has been killed? Radio Basilisk reported it. And you're a suspect."

"I'm very sorry, Madame."

"Why don't you hand yourself in? And look at the state of you. You look completely bedraggled. You urgently need a bath."

"What I need is wine and sleep."

"Come on," Hunkeler interjected. "Sit down. Tomorrow we'll decide what to do."

"To your health, Madame," said Moor. "And thank you for your hospitality."

Hedwig sat down and took a gulp.

"What a business, my God."

She looked at Estelle.

"And you? Don't you think it's terrible what's going on here?"

"*Mais non*," Estelle replied. "Not at all. It's quite exciting."

It was midnight and Hunkeler was sitting alone in the kitchen. He drank several glasses of water and smoked a cigarette.

He'd put Moor to bed. The man had been as heavy as a sack of potatoes as he'd dragged him up the stairs and forced him to undress and slip into a nightshirt. Then he'd cleared the kitchen table and put the empty bottles to the side. There were four. Moor had drunk himself into a stupor.

When he'd finished the cigarette, he got up and chucked the butt into the stove, where a few embers were still aglow. He stepped over to the open window and looked out. The light from the kitchen illuminated the grass as far as the cherry tree. To either side left and right it was pitch-black. And above was complete darkness too. No moon, no stars. A gentle wind could be heard as it rippled through the branches of the trees. It came from the west, it would rain soon.

He thought about Hedwig and how lucky he was to have her. She'd only been cross for a short while after she'd arrived. Then, in her characteristically pragmatic manner, she'd accepted Moor's presence as something that couldn't be changed that night. And whatever he decided to do over the coming days, he knew she wouldn't strongly oppose him. She trusted Hunkeler to know what he was doing. And sooner or later, he was certain, it would transpire that Moor wasn't the perpetrator.

Hunkeler listened out for other night-time sounds apart from the wind. There was usually something to be heard at this time of night. The distant revving of a motorbike. An owl calling out in the darkness. A hedgehog searching for snails and slugs in the grass. Nothing. All he could hear was the wind brushing past.

There were no sounds from within the house either. No marten scampering across the attic floor, no creaking from a wooden beam. All was quiet.

He went into the hallway and dialled Lüdi's private number. Lüdi was generally still awake at this hour, waiting for a call from his boyfriend in Paris.

"*Oui, mon joujou?*" Lüdi whispered.

"I'm not your *joujou*, I'm your former colleague Hunkeler."

"Oh. Hang on a sec."

He heard Lüdi tapping a cigarette out of the packet, followed by the clicking of a lighter.

"What's up? But keep it short, I'm expecting a call."

"Is there any news on Meierhans?"

Lüdi laughed. It sounded more like a snigger, but he always sounded like that.

"That's a good one. You know I'm not allowed to say anything."

"Oh, come on. I promise I won't pass it on."

More sniggering, then two deep drags on the cigarette.

"Why do you want to know?"

"Because old Moor is here with me. And because Bardet was here. He's looking for him, even though he agrees it wasn't Moor."

"Are you crazy? Why are you doing this to yourself?"

Hunkeler didn't reply to that.

"OK then, because it's you," Lüdi continued. "Madörin has a strong lead. It doesn't relate to Moor. Happy now?"

"Wait, don't hang up yet. What's the situation with Viktor Waldmeier? Do they know anything more?"

"Officially, nothing is known."

"And unofficially?"

"People are saying he'll be released soon. On a bail payment of ten million dollars."

"Who says that?"

"Someone with good connections to New York."

Hunkeler was thinking feverishly.

"If Waldmeier is going to be released, then it must mean that he's prepared to work with the Americans. That he's going to plead guilty and spill the beans," Hunkeler speculated. "Then the Volksbank will come under enormous pressure. In an extreme case, it might be excluded from the American market and face insolvency. Then Basel City would have to bail it out, as per state guarantee."

A brief sniggering from Lüdi.

"That's exactly what Antoinette Oser of the Liberal faction pressed for in parliament yesterday. She requested a unanimous declaration from the governing council that the capital is secure, that the state will step in."

"And? Has the council done that?"

More clicking of the lighter. Lüdi, who never smoked during the day, evidently turned into a chain-smoker at night.

"Not yet. But they will do soon. They have no choice."

"Jesus!"

"Anything else?"

"No. Good night. And thank you, sweetie pie."

Hunkeler stepped to the open window and drew the night air deep into his lungs. There was a patter, soft and gentle. The rain had set in. From further up the valley came the call of an owl, several times in succession. And very close by, up in the poplar, another owl replied.

Two days later Hunkeler couldn't bear it any more. Old Moor was no bother at all. He just sat in the kitchen with a bottle of wine and didn't say a word. At night he slept in the barn, where Hunkeler had sorted out a bed for him. Moor said he preferred sleeping there, he didn't need to climb any stairs and he felt less confined.

Estelle, on the other hand, had turned out to be a real pest. Wherever Hunkeler went, she always came along. She constantly wanted to talk to him, except when she was on the phone. Fortunately that was often the case.

She had been determined to go out for a walk – with Hunkeler and the goat. He declined. He wasn't going to make himself a laughing stock in the village. A goat isn't a dog, he told her. So she went on her own, with the goat on a rope. She came back after two hours, completely worn out. Madame Lucie had refused to walk any further than the last house. No amount of pulling had helped, she had simply bucked.

Hunkeler decided to find Estelle a job, as quickly as possible. Knowing she'd previously worked in a bar, he thought of the Alte Grenze. It was an alternative place, they were used to young folk there.

He got in the car and took the route over Knoeringue. At the Stollers' inn, he parked up and went inside. The restaurant was still empty, as usual just before lunchtime. He sat down at the regulars' table and ordered coffee. He could hear Frau Stoller at work in the kitchen.

After a while, Frau Stoller appeared and briefly sat down beside him. "How is Christian?" she asked.

Hunkeler hesitated before answering. "As far as I've heard, he's not doing too badly," he replied. "It's probably for the best if he hides himself away for a while."

"Yes, I agree. A Monsieur Bardet was here, from Mulhouse. He was looking for Christian. They searched the house and had a quick look in the barn. But they didn't seem that determined to find anything."

She stood up. "*Je m'excuse*, but I've got to get back to work. Are you staying for lunch? I'm doing cordon bleu."

"No, sorry. Just one more question. Was anyone here from Basel, yesterday or the day before?"

"Yes, of course. We live off the customers from Basel. The usual crowd was here for dinner."

"I was thinking more of the afternoon. And the morning."

She thought for a while, then nodded. "The day before yesterday, an older man was here in the morning. He comes by quite regularly. I think he buys vegetables from the organic farm in Franken. He has strikingly long hair, in a plait. I think he's a cook."

"When was that exactly?"

"A little after nine. Whether he was on his way there or on his way back I don't know. He had a coffee and then went off for a walk. He was gone about an hour. I know because he left his car here. He usually walks along the Roman road."

"And apart from him? Was anyone else here?"

"Yes, yesterday, around the same time. A stocky, beefy-looking man. Like you, he asked if anyone had been here. He was pretty arrogant."

"And did you tell him about the man with the long plait?"

"Yes, of course. I didn't mean any harm. Have I done something wrong?"

"No, I don't think so. What car was he driving?"

"Well, I don't usually pay attention to that sort of thing. But with him I did have a look. It was a red Fiat. It's a pity you can't stay for food. I'd have more time after."

She hesitated. There was obviously something else she wanted to say.

"I would like to give my regards to Christian. If you happen to come across him."

"That's quite possible, who knows."

Hunkeler carried on driving along Hohe Strasse towards the Rhine. Leaden clouds hung low from the sky and a heavy rain set in, hammering down onto the car roof. The Black Forest and the Jura Mountains were completely obscured. Only the lights of the airport down on the plain were visible, shimmering through the spray.

He was reflecting on what Frau Stoller had said. Paul Egloff, the old anarchist, had evidently stopped off in Knoeringue on Thursday. It was good to know he was around. Hunkeler wanted to ask him about a job for Estelle. The stocky, beefy-looking man had to be Madörin. He drove a red Fiat. He was probably following another one of his red-hot leads.

Hunkeler grinned. There was no helping Madörin. Nor did Hunkeler want to help him. It wasn't his problem any more. Let him run down yet another blind alley in his determination to uncover a conspiracy.

He stared fixedly at the road, which was awash with rain. Moor weather, it occurred to him. If Moor were still painting, he would be mixing up different shades of grey on his palette now, finely nuanced graduations of dark and light, as he had done all his life. But how could you carry on painting when you'd lost everything – wife, house, and customers who used to look at the paintings and occasionally buy one? How else to cope than to watch as the fire devoured all the shades of grey?

Hunkeler was still driving in second gear, not just because of the slippery road. He needed to let his mind settle before he could think clearly. The last few days had been frenetic. First Estelle, then the goat, then Moor. He probably should have sent all three of them away. He wasn't used to sharing his home with others any more. Apart from Hedwig, but that was different.

He thought of the phone conversation with Lüdi yesterday evening. It had unsettled him. The Americans were obviously in the process of bringing the venerable Swiss Confederation to its knees. And without firing a single shot.

When he was young, thought Hunkeler, the Swiss had been proud of their country. People spoke of the free Swiss citizen and were referring to themselves. People were proud that refugees were being granted asylum. And people were also proud of the banks, where the money of innocent people who faced persecution was held in safety. A little bit of the freedom fighter William Tell was in every Swiss citizen.

But today you almost had to be ashamed of being Swiss. The asylum policy during the Second World War was now known to have been racist. The once highly esteemed banks were having to pay gigantic fines. And bankers were being made to confess their guilt in American courts as if they were the subject of some kind of Stalinist show trial.

Was it even still permitted to be a free Swiss citizen? Or was it forbidden to live in a small, sovereign country in the middle of Europe, a country which made its own laws?

It was Switzerland's fate, he thought, to have been spared. Even in the Thirty Years War, almost four hundred years ago, it had been spared when the villages burned in Alsace. The Swiss saw the fires burn and the idiom 'to see the fire in Alsace' became a fixed phrase in the local dialect. It was spared in the First World War, when 30,000 German and French soldiers shot each other to death on Hartmannswillerkopf in the southern Vosges mountains. And it was spared in the Second World War, when 22,000 people starved to death or were barbarically murdered in the Struthof concentration camp west of Strasbourg, not far from the gates of peaceful Basel.

People wanted to believe they'd been spared because they had been particularly capable and clever. But the truth was that being spared always carried with it a degree of guilt. The guilt of not suffering the same fate and of profiting from the suffering of others. Some wise people recognized this truth and spoke out. But nobody wanted to hear about it. The fact that some of the nation's banks prospered exorbitantly and took in vast amounts of money from all over the world was noted, first with incredulity and astonishment, then with growing satisfaction. Surely that couldn't be a bad thing – they were confederate banks after all. Confederate meant "in fidelity and faith". The nimbus of the old people's assemblies in which the men stood together under open skies and voted by show of hands on which laws to adopt, this nimbus also surrounded the bank vaults shielded from public view. Vaults in which money from all manner of origins was hidden and profitably invested. This worked out fine for a while. The capable, clever and dutiful Swiss swarmed out across the world with their bulging money bags and spread their towels under the palms of the most beautiful beaches.

Until the data of those bank vaults was hacked and the banks were exposed as dealers in stolen goods. That was the end of being spared. The guilt had caught up with the spared. Switzerland lost its special status and became an ordinary country, like all the other countries – not an ideal state shaped by noble convictions, but a syndicate that fought shrewdly and fiercely for its own interests and advantage.

These were the bitter thoughts of retired detective inspector Peter Hunkeler as he reached the former garrison town of Huningue in torrential rain. He rolled across the main square on which Napoleon's soldiers had once paraded. This was where the French had brought Bern's state treasure in 1798, after they'd taken control of the old, proud city of Bern and had raided the noblemen's cellars. Five heavy carriages drawn by four horses each were required to carry the weight of all that silver and gold, as Hunkeler had once read. The thought still filled him with secret glee, for as well as being Swiss, he was also an Aargau man. And the part of Aargau in which he grew up had been subjugated by the lords and rulers of Bern for centuries.

He parked by the Rhine and headed for the footbridge that led across to the German town of Weil. Shielded by his umbrella, he walked to the middle of the bridge and stopped there. The river was swollen, as usual in April. Brown waves surged northwards, down towards the sea. On the left he could see the silo towers of the Rhine port, to the right the village church of Huningue. Behind it stood the high-rise blocks of Basel's pharmaceutical giants. The historic centre of Basel with its church towers wasn't visible, the rainfall was too heavy.

Turning around, he followed the river downstream until he reached the campsite Paul Egloff had told him about. Around three dozen caravans stood there, many with awnings, camping tables and plastic flowers. He saw a woman sitting under one of the awnings. She seemed to be listening to the rain drumming down. "Come on over," she said. "Don't be scared, I don't bite. Take a seat, keep me company for a while."

He went over and sat down. She looked to be well into her seventies. She was wearing a winter coat and had pink dyed hair.

"I can't offer you any coffee, I'm afraid. The gas bottle is empty. I feel cold all day long. And in the night. Here are some cookies, help yourself. I assume you don't want to know my name. It's irrelevant anyway. I'm spending my retirement here, in case you're interested."

She tried to laugh. He popped a cookie into his mouth.

"Don't be shy, young man. I've got more inside. Tell me a story. Something about desire and adventure. I love listening to stories. Stories about sailors who are swallowed by the sea. About mariners who encounter mermaids and are pulled down to a watery grave. But I only want the truth, the bona fide truth. And no happy end. Happy endings are a lie. Don't you think?"

She hadn't taken her eyes off him for a single second since he'd sat down. She was watching his every move.

"And the lady?" she asked as he shoved a cigarette between his lips.

"Pardon me, Madame," Hunkeler replied. "Ladies first." He offered her one and held out the lighter for her.

"Thank you, good sir," she said.

From out on the river came the drone of an engine. A ship was pounding its way up the Rhine. A little later they heard the waves splash against the shore.

"That's a tanker," she told him. "Probably the *Tristan*. It sails under a Dutch flag and travels all the way up to Schweizerhalle port. It will get unloaded there. That happens really fast these days. Towards evening it will come back down. More quietly though, it'll be on an empty run. If you want, we can wait together until we hear it again."

She smiled at him and threw her cigarette butt out into the rain.

"But you don't want to, of course. It's too boring for you. You should come in summer, on a hot evening, when they all flock out here from Basel. To the cool river, because it's too hot in the city to sleep. Then it's party time here."

She looked at him provocatively.

"I used to know everyone who travelled past here. I was at the helm myself, for forty years. I knew all the bakers and butchers who docked alongside the barge. The port bars. And the beautiful port girls. I was one of them myself."

She took her gaze off him and looked over to the alder trees.

"I assume you've come about Egloff."

Hunkeler was taken aback, but he didn't show it.

"Why do you assume that?"

"Because he was arrested yesterday evening. At the Alte Grenze in Basel. Didn't you know?"

No, he hadn't known.

"Helga Seiler, the landlady at the Alte Grenze, was here early this morning. She told me. Arrested on suspicion of murder. So stupid. Paul couldn't hurt a fly. Helga took a few things from Paul's caravan."

"What kind of things?"

"Books, articles, stuff like that. I've no idea what they were about. And shortly after, Monsieur Wirz from the St Louis gendarmerie turned up, with two men I didn't know. They searched Paul's caravan and then sealed it. Another idiocy. As if the door couldn't simply be forced open. His caravan is over there, under the alders."

She raised her hand, revealing her skinny arm.

"I feel sorry for the guy. I like him, even though he has that disgusting long plait. It's completely matted, no hope of getting a comb through that. He probably hasn't washed it in years. But that's how he is, Paul. Once he's decided on something, he follows it through. He says anarchy is the only way forward these days if we want to stop the world from falling apart. He told me the global electronic system can only lead to catastrophe, because it fundamentally contradicts nature. Living nature produces life, electronics produce destruction and death. I can remember those sentences because they made an impression on me. He's good at explaining it all. He said that's why he doesn't pay any bills from the council or the state. Because he rejects the system. He said refusing to fund the system that is destroying the world is the only way to destroy the system itself. That's another sentence that stayed with me. Well, that's Paul for you, absolutely resolute. But he's certainly no murderer. He always goes to get me a new gas bottle when the old one is empty. He pays for it, he knows I don't have any money. Now I'm hoping he'll be back again soon. Then I can offer you a coffee next time you come. You are going to come and visit me again, Monsieur, aren't you?"

Hunkeler stood up.

"Thank you, Madame. You've helped me a lot."

The woman attempted a mischievous smile.

"What with, Monsieur?"


As he left the caravan site he saw a red car parked over by the plane trees. It looked familiar, very familiar. He immediately averted his gaze and carried on walking without slowing his step. Then he glanced across once more. The car was parked behind two trees which almost entirely hid it from view. It was a Fiat. And it had a Basel licence plate.

Hunkeler lowered the umbrella over his head and walked away briskly to get out of the wet. At the corner he turned off towards the main square. He knew a good bakery there that also sold cheese. He was going to buy a baguette and a Camembert. A fresh baguette with ripe Camembert was an absolute joy.

Madörin, that bastard, he thought as he left the bakery. Arresting Egloff had undoubtedly been his idea. He obviously had his sights on a specific type of perpetrator in the Meierhans case: the anarchists.

Anyway, what business did he have, snooping around in France? None whatsoever. Searching Egloff's caravan was the responsibility of the St Louis gendarmerie. And it was Commissaire Bardet in Mulhouse who was in charge of the Philipp Meierhans case.

But Hunkeler had no business being on the caravan park in Huningue either. The police forces on both sides of the border were hypersensitive to unauthorized interference from the opposite side. Much was always made of their excellent transborder collaboration, but if it came out that a former Basel inspector had been sniffing around on a French caravan site, alarm bells would ring in St Louis and Mulhouse. The fact that he'd only come to ask Paul Egloff whether there might be any work for Estelle at the Alte Grenze would make little difference. He should have probably driven straight back to his house and gone for a stroll with Madame Lucie.

He hunkered down under the tautly stretched cloth of the umbrella and walked back towards the Rhine through the rain. He kept to the cover of the plane trees and then quickly crossed the road to the first caravan. Here he waited and listened. The only sound was the drumming of the rain. After a while he peered round the corner. He glimpsed Madörin to the left, three caravans along. He was standing motionlessly under an awning, barely noticeable, his gaze focused on the alders by the river bank.

Sure enough, the guy was staking out Egloff's caravan, he even had a pair of binoculars in his hands. Madörin briefly raised them to his eyes, but nothing was moving over there by the alders.

Hunkeler retreated and quickly walked to his car. He started the engine as smoothly as possible and rolled away quietly. As he drove across the main square of Huningue he breathed a sigh of relief. He was fairly certain Madörin had seen him when he was sitting outside the old woman's caravan. But he also felt certain that Madörin had no idea he himself had been seen by Hunkeler.

\*

He drove through the industrial estate occupied by the Swiss pharmaceutical giants, who had relocated some of their facilities over here into the EU country of France. After the border he merged with the slow-moving traffic on the city bypass. Basel was full of construction sites, on every crossroads, at every traffic light.

At Burgfelderstrasse he turned off right and parked. He was outside the Alte Grenze, a mighty building with granite block foundations. It had once been a popular bar, with music and dance every Saturday evening. Later, when every household had a television, the inn had faded into a dive for drunks. Then, in the eighties, it had become a cooperatively owned establishment. Hunkeler often stopped off here. He liked Helga Seiler, the landlady, and he loved the simple food they served.

A sign by the door announced it was closed today. As the lights were on inside, he went in anyway. The place was empty, except for Helga Seiler, who was sitting at one of the tables. "Are you another one of them?" she barked. "Are you lot completely insane?"

"Why?" he asked. "Are the police here?"

"They're back there, in the office. They're searching everything. I'm not allowed in there any more."

Hunkeler laid the baguette and Camembert on the table and walked down the hallway to the back. He found Police Constable Schaub standing outside a door.

"You here, Inspector? I thought you'd retired."

"I have. I'm here purely by coincidence. And I'm wondering whether you've all gone raving mad."

"Don't say that, Inspector. There's heavily incriminating evidence against one of the cooks who works here. This may be a hotbed of conspiracy. At least that's what Madörin says. We're just doing our duty."

"What evidence?"

Schaub stepped closer to Hunkeler and whispered: "The cook Paul Egloff was seen in Knoeringue the day before yesterday. At the same time as Philipp Meierhans was murdered."

"Don't talk nonsense. It's not even clear whether it was murder or manslaughter. Or an accident."

Schaub looked disconcerted. Hunkeler was still a person of authority for him.

"There's other evidence."

"For example?"

"The articles Egloff read and wrote. I've heard he's calling for violent resistance against the banks. We can't have that. We all keep our money in the banks. A person like that is a threat to society."

"Well then, Constable Schaub, thank you for your report," Hunkeler replied in a sharp voice. "Carry on doing your duty."

"Yes, Inspector."

Hunkeler returned to the front, sat down opposite Helga and broke off a piece of the baguette.

"A glass of house white please. And a knife for the cheese."

"I'm not in the mood for jokes," said Helga.

"I'm not joking. I'm hungry and I want to eat with you." He winked at her.

Helga went and fetched some wine and two glasses. There was a loud crunch as Hunkeler sank his teeth into the fresh bread.

"Wonderful. A baguette has a shelf life of half a day. That's how long it stays crisp for. After that you can give it to the pigs. So come on, let's tuck in."

His enthusiasm was infectious, she decided to join in.

"By the way, I wanted to ask whether you might have any work for my granddaughter," he said. "She's eighteen and pretty smart. She has waitressing experience."

"We might have. Once this nightmare here is over. I'd have to meet her first."

Police Constable Schaub appeared behind the bar and looked on as they ate.

"Sorry, Schaub," said Hunkeler. "It's absolutely delicious and I'd happily invite you to join us, but you know the drill."

"I'm on duty, boss. But thanks anyway." Schaub retreated back down the hallway.

"So what's the story with Egloff and Knoeringue?" Hunkeler quietly asked.

"The day before yesterday, he wanted to buy vegetables at the organic farm in Franken. He took my car. There was no one around at the farm, so he drove back and stopped for coffee in Knoeringue. Then he went for a short walk along the Roman road. That's all."

"And those articles? What's all that about?"

"He's written a couple of pieces for a magazine published in Germany. He gave them to me to look at. They read quite well. He has a nice theory on how to save the world, but there's no incitement to violence."

"Perhaps he decided to take action after all. Meierhans was an important banker. And to anarchists, bankers are the epitome of evil."

"Nonsense. They're just a small group of disparate idealists."

Hunkeler would have liked to ask her more, but then the door opened and Madörin walked in. He briefly took stock of the room with a measured gaze. Then he walked over to their table and struck a pose, legs apart, shoulders hunched forward, chin jutting out. "What are you doing here?" he demanded.

"Eating, as you can see. Unfortunately there's not much left, otherwise I'd happily invite you."

"Unauthorized entry into locked premises, obstructing the work of the forensic department, interfering in an ongoing investigation. Do you want to hear more?"

"Not true. The door wasn't locked, the forensic department is still hard at work in the office and I'm not interfering."

"Then why are you here?"

"For purely personal reasons. I'm looking for a job for my granddaughter."

"Since when have you got a granddaughter?"

"Since eighteen years ago. She's going to work here as a waitress."

"That's right, I'm going to employ her," Helga Seiler confirmed. "Can I get you a coffee?"

Hunkeler shoved a chair towards Madörin. "Sit down and take the weight off a while. We're old colleagues, after all. And most of the time we worked together well, didn't we?"

"All right then," Madörin replied and sat down.

"So, how are you?" Hunkeler asked cheerily. "How's business?"

Madörin mournfully shook his head. He was exhausted. He evidently hadn't had much sleep the past few nights. "I don't know what's the matter with you," he said as he stirred three sugars into his coffee. "Why won't you learn? You could be having a lovely time in your house in Alsace, you've earned it. But instead you keep meddling in things that don't concern you any more. You know that's not allowed."

He shook his head again, slowly, disillusioned.

"I learned a lot from you. And I still like you, despite everything. But there comes a time when one has to let go. I wonder why you're not able to do that."

Madörin took a gulp of his coffee, then he drained the cup.

"We've been contacted by the St Louis gendarmerie, they said you were hanging around on the caravan site in Huningue earlier today. Near Egloff's caravan."

"Is that so? Who rang you?"

Madörin shot him a short sharp glance, then he lowered his gaze.

"Gendarme Wirz."

"Oh him. Well, if he says I was there, then I probably was."

"Is that all you can say? You know I have to report this. The gendarmerie is bound to raise hell over it."

"Why don't we wait and see? Who knows what else Wirz might decide to share."

Another quick glance, venomous, but not so self-assured any more.

"What do you mean, wait and see?"

"It's true that I was there. But not because of Egloff's arrest. I didn't even know about that. I only found out from the old woman. Interestingly, I couldn't help notice as I left that your car was parked under the plane trees. And when I turned to take a closer look I saw you standing under an awning with a pair of binoculars in your hands. A Basel inspector carrying out surveillance in Huningue without the gendarmerie's knowledge? What's going on?"

The colour drained from Madörin's face. He sat motionless for a moment, then he stood up abruptly and walked out without a word.

"My goodness," said Helga Seiler. "Worse than in a kindergarten."

"Stuff him," said Hunkeler. "One–nil to me. Cheers."

Hunkeler drove to his apartment on Mittlere Strasse and parked. It had stopped raining and the asphalt was gleaming in the sunlight. The wisteria that grew all the way up to the roof of the neighbouring house was in full flower. The smell was heavenly, it reminded him of Italy.

He decided to pay a visit to the flea market on Petersplatz. He felt better than he had in a long time. Madörin the bastard, he'd shown him. That lousy, scheming scumbag. Thought he could trick him with his lie about Gendarme Wirz. But not with him, not with Hunkeler. He was still the top dog.

He walked along the tree-lined Bernoullistrasse, past the university library. To his left lay the manicured gardens of venerable old town houses. The afternoon sunshine had brought people out and the flea market on Petersplatz was still in full swing. Stalls were lined up in groups of four, old clothes, baby equipment, vinyl records. The air below the branches of the tall elms was thick with the smell of cheese tarts, bratwurst and candied almonds. Young people were promenading among the stalls, examining items, enquiring about the price. Men from North Africa, women from the Balkans and Turkey, bartering hard despite their limited knowledge of German.

By the corner near the university entrance stood a van with an Alsatian licence plate. One of the sides was folded down and served as a sales counter. Old music boxes were arranged on it. Inside the vehicle, various knick-knacks were displayed on shelves. A man of about fifty sat at a camping table in front of the van, drinking tea from a small cup. Hunkeler stared at him.

"What's the matter, Monsieur?" the man asked. "Why are you looking at me like that? Are you from the police?"

"No, but I have a question," Hunkeler replied. "Where are you from?"

"Morocco. Why? Do we know each other?"

Hunkeler felt rather stupid now. He would have liked to turn tail and flee, but it was too late for that.

"No. I'm just wondering where you got all these beautiful things from. And where you learned to speak German so fluently."

"I lived in Berlin for a few years. Now I live in Alsace. But I'm not sure that's any of your business."

Hunkeler picked up one of the music boxes. "This is very pretty. What melody does it play?"

The man activated the mechanism. A musette waltz, light and delicate, rose from the box.

"I'll take it. How much does it cost?"

The price was outrageously high, in Hunkeler's opinion. But he paid without hesitating.

The man slid the music box into a small bag and gave him a card with his address. *Mustafa Barikla, Les Prés*. It was him. "In case something breaks," he said, pointing at the card. "I can repair it."

"Thank you. Have a good afternoon." Hunkeler wanted to get away, as fast as possible.

"But Monsieur, it would be very rude of you to leave without drinking some tea with me. Please, sit down. We'll do it like in the bazaars."

Hunkeler sat down on a folding chair which nearly collapsed under his weight and watched the man pour the tea.

"I also sell goat's cheese from the Vosges mountains, in case you're interested. Best quality and organic. Do you want to try some?"

"No thanks. But I'll take four pieces if you can wrap them."

"With pleasure. Cheers. Here's to a long, trouble-free life."

Hunkeler drained his cup. It was strongly sweetened peppermint tea.

"You look familiar somehow," the man said. "Don't we know each other from somewhere?"

"Where from? No, I don't think so."

Hunkeler was about to stand up when he saw a young, delicate woman walk past. She was wearing a blue headscarf. She briefly looked at him, she had greenish-grey eyes. He knew those eyes, he would never forget them, and it was clear she'd recognized him too. She hurriedly walked on.

"Wait," Hunkeler called out. "Don't walk away. I need to talk to you." He tried to jump up and almost fell over. "Wait, Mademoiselle, please," he called after her.

He wasn't fast enough. He saw her disappear into the crowd.

"Are you OK?" the man asked. "You've gone very pale."

"Yes, yes, I'm fine."

Hunkeler grabbed the little bag and thought about running after her, but he decided not to. He knew she was long gone.

"Have another cup of tea," the man suggested as he

took him by the arm. "You don't happen to have a house in Alsace?"

"Perhaps I do," Hunkeler growled. "We'll talk some other time."

He walked back along Mittlere Strasse. His surroundings seemed unreal and dreamlike, as if he was in a daze. An ordinary suburban road, built more than a hundred years ago, that ran straight as a die towards Kannenfeld Park and Alsace. It was a sought-after residential area, quiet, and yet you could reach the market square on foot in ten minutes. He knew some of his neighbours, but just in passing. He always greeted them politely when he encountered anyone. But he still didn't feel properly at home here. He missed the trees, the landscape, the far-reaching views.

Now this familiar reality seemed to him like an opaque screen behind which a different image appeared, and though vague, it had an inescapable intensity. A young woman standing motionlessly, observing the face of the dying Stephan Fankhauser as he gasped for air. He tried to erase the image, to push it aside. To concentrate on the street he was walking along. On the rusty bars of the garden fence to his right, behind which a small, overgrown park offered occasional glimpses of a white house. It was the only part of Mittlere Strasse that wasn't entirely built up. He took in the smell of damp grass and wondered who lived in this house.

Hunkeler felt a dizziness come over him and had to hold onto the iron bars with both hands to keep himself upright.

He could feel his pulse in his throat. It was racing, even though he hadn't overexerted himself in the least. He took a deep breath, then gently breathed out again.

He slowly carried on walking. Like a puppet hanging on strings, it occurred to him. Guided by an unknown, invisible hand. He tried to take firm steps, to ground himself on the asphalt under his feet.

When he picked up the scent of the wisteria, its captivating realness made him feel better. He sat down on the low wall in front of the eye hospital, took out his handkerchief and wiped his face. It was dripping with sweat. What had befallen him just then? A panic attack? Was he a case for the loony bin?

He looked across at the lilac blossom that hung in bunches, filling the entire street with its scent – unexpectedly exotic, a promise from the south. The blooms were spread across the building's entire facade, encircling balconies and windows. The house next door contained the apartment he had lived in for decades.

It wasn't the encounter with his son-in-law that had made him feel as though the ground had fallen from under his feet, he reflected. That encounter was one he'd sought out, otherwise he wouldn't have gone to the flea market. And Mustafa Barikla seemed to be a sound guy. No concerns there, except for the religious differences. But that wasn't really any of his business. It was simply like that these days, people loved each other across cultures.

No, it was seeing the young woman with the headscarf that had shaken him so much. The quick, precise look she had shot him, and the immediate recognition. Her flight into the throng of people, even though she had undoubtedly heard him call. But she didn't want to talk to him. Didn't want him to ask her what had happened that night at the hospital. And he'd been too slow.

He felt very old as he sat there on the low wall and looked across to his apartment. Frail, heading for gradual disintegration. But there was something he still wanted to achieve. He wanted to find out why the young woman had run away from him. What secret was she hiding?

Twenty minutes later Hunkeler pulled up outside his house in Alsace. He could hear the milking machine running in the shed across the road. There was no sign of Estelle, nor of Moor. When he entered the kitchen he saw a note on the table: *Have tied Lucie to the walnut tree. Am visiting a friend. Love and kisses, Estelle.*

He went back out the front. There was no goat tied to the walnut tree. But he did hear a cheerful bleating. It was coming from across the road, from his neighbour's vegetable garden. Lucie was standing in it, eating the last few remaining seedlings with visible delight.

"You damned animal," growled Hunkeler. He slowly approached the goat to try and catch her. But she had other ideas. She wanted to skip and jump. It took some doing before he finally managed to grab hold of the rope. "That's enough leaping about for now," he told her. "Come on, into the shed with you. And if you behave you can go for a walk every now and then."

He dragged her off the vegetable patch and into his neighbour's milking shed. His neighbour watched with puzzlement as he yanked the stubborn animal to a free space at the feed trough and tied it up.

"I'm sorry," he said. "You're going to have to replant. The bloody animal has eaten all the seedlings."

"Has she? The little pest!" Then she laughed heartily. "She knows what's good, *n'est-ce pas?* That's goats for you, inquisitive and cheeky."

"I bought her on the market in Altkirch, off a woman from Jettingen. I'm going to take her back tomorrow."

"That's not necessary. She can stay here. As long as she behaves. I've got plenty of milk, and there's always something to laugh about with a goat."

"Thank you very much. I'll pay for any expenses, of course. And for the seedlings."

"*D'accord,* we'll do it like that."

He was about to take his leave when he realized there was something else on her mind. He sat down on the bench.

"My niece in Knoeringue rang me," she said after a while. "The Krotzer lad tried to hang himself. *Ufhänke, ufem Dachbode,* in their attic. His mother noticed something wasn't right. She went to look for him. He already had the rope around his neck."

She looked at him with sad eyes.

"*Sone junge Maa.* Such a young man, it's terrible. Something needs to be done, surely?"

Hunkeler thought for a while. What could be done?

"How old is he, the Krotzers' lad?"

"His name is René. He's not even eighteen yet."

"Then he will fall under juvenile law. As far as I know that's no different in France. He should hand himself in."

135

"He refuses to. He says it's not his fault that a shot went off."

"He needs to tell that to the police. They'll investigate it. If he doesn't have the courage to hand himself in, his mother should call them. It's important they do it, and as soon as possible."

"You're a police officer. Can't you help?"

"No. I have to keep out of it. Otherwise I'll get into trouble."

"Because of Monsieur Moor?"

"Yes, also because of Monsieur Moor."

"*Bon*, I will get word to his mother that she needs to contact them," she said.


When Hunkeler left the milking shed he saw a delivery van with an Alsatian licence plate parked outside his house. He recognized it immediately, it was Mustafa Barikla's van. The door to the barn was open. Hunkeler could hear men shouting in there.

He crossed the road and went to see what was going on. Mustafa was sitting on the floor, leaning against an old oil drum. His hands were raised to his head, which was bleeding. Next to him stood Moor with a roof batten in his hand.

"Are you crazy?" Hunkeler asked. "Have you both gone stark raving mad?"

"The bastard thumped me with a batten, *le salaud*," said Barikla. "I didn't see him because I'd just stepped in from the bright daylight. He ambushed me."

"What's he doing here?" Moor asked. "He has no business snooping around in here. Who is he anyway?"

"This is Mustafa Barikla, you idiot," Hunkeler barked at him. "Estelle's father."

"How was I supposed to know that? To me he was an unknown intruder. A gendarme looking for me."

"The guy is a thug," said Barikla. "He nearly smashed my brains in."

"Right, enough of this," Hunkeler ordered. "Come into the kitchen and I'll bandage up the wound."

They went inside and Hunkeler fetched the first aid kit. "It's a laceration, that's all," he said. "It'll heal soon enough." He wrapped a gauze bandage round Mustafa's head. "Anyway, why did you come here, Mustafa?" he asked him.

"Are we on first-name terms then?" Barikla replied.

"Well of course, since you're my son-in-law."

"*Bon.* Pleased to meet you, *beau-père.*"

"Hang on, not so fast. It's Pierre to you."

"*D'accord*, fine with me, Pierre. So where's Estelle? I thought she was here."

Hunkeler pointed at the note lying on the table. "Read for yourself. Visiting a friend."

"So, in Mulhouse then. It's enough to drive you mad. She does whatever she wants."

"Well, what do you suggest? Should she do whatever she doesn't want?"

That made Barikla laugh. "No, of course not, Pierre." He put the plastic bag he'd been holding all that time on the table. "I just wanted to bring you the goat's cheese."

"I see. And why didn't you come to the house, instead of going into the barn?"

"Because I didn't have the courage to knock on your door. You were so unfriendly at the market."

"Rubbish. We traded politely, we drank tea together. And I paid far too much for that music box, by the way."

"*Mais non.* They're valuable objects and very sought after."

"Nonsense. And I can buy goat's cheese in the cheese shop for half the price."

"But not of this quality. This is pure nature. Our goats eat only the best herbs."

"How about a drop of wine?" Moor asked.

"OK," said Hunkeler and fetched a bottle.

"And you, Mustafa, are you joining us?"

"Yes, why not. Thanks."

"But aren't you a Muslim?"

"More or less in the same way as this thug here is a Christian. He's supposed to love his enemies, but instead he nearly cracked my skull."

"OK, wine all round. Let's drink to good health," said Hunkeler.

Shortly before midnight, Hunkeler rang Hedwig. "Yes?" she mumbled.

"It's me, Peter. Did I wake you?"

"No, I've only just got into bed."

"Mustafa was here."

She yawned lazily. "I know."

"What? Who from?"

"Isabelle. She rang me and we talked about it."

"Why does nobody tell me anything?" he shouted.

"I told you just now. That Moor, he seems to be a real hooligan. Bit of a loose cannon. How much longer is he going to be staying at the house?"

"Not much longer. He's harmless, he only wanted to defend himself. Well then, sleep tight."

"Wait, don't hang up yet," she said. There was another long yawn. "Isabelle has invited us."

"How do you mean, invited us?"

"To her house in the Vosges mountains."

He didn't say anything to that.

"Are you still there?"

"Yes. But why has she invited us?"

"Heavens, you really are the most impossible guy I've ever come across. Aren't you happy?"

"I don't know. First I don't hear anything from her for years, then she suddenly invites us."

He heard Hedwig laugh. "You're funny. You get on OK with Estelle and Mustafa, don't you?"

"Well, yes. And when is this visit supposed to happen?"

"After Easter, early May."

He hesitated, but he couldn't very well turn the invitation down.

"All right. It's a way off yet."

"So is that settled then?"

"I said all right."

"It'll be nice. We'll all be together. Sleep tight, Peter."

On Monday morning Hunkeler drove along Hohe Strasse towards Basel. Prosecutor Suter had personally called and asked him to join their crisis meeting at three o'clock at Waaghof station.

"It's all hands to the pumps. Red alert. We're in a terrible fix. I need every man on board."

"I've been discharged, I'm not part of the crew any more. I'm old and stupid."

Hunkeler heard Suter exhaling sharply through the nose, as if he was trying to chase away an irritating insect.

"Please refrain from making such eccentric assertions. We need your expertise. You were part of the 1968 protest movement."

"Only peripherally. I was a hanger-on."

"But you know what it was all about. What kind of people were these revolutionaries? What drove them? What are their thoughts on it now?"

"Glorious days of youth. Long gone and forgotten."

Again the sharp exhalation. Suter was in a sulk.

"Commissaire Bardet will be there too. I'm appealing to your sense of responsibility towards the city of Basel, your solidarity with your former colleagues. I'm counting on your attendance."

Hunkeler grinned to himself somewhat gleefully as he drove past Trois Maisons. He couldn't help gloat. The prosecutor must be up to his neck in it if he deigned to make a call like that and had to draw on the support of a veteran inspector. Evidently this inspector didn't yet belong on the scrapheap after all.

He looked across at Estelle, who was sitting next to him in the car. She was in a real huff. They were on their way to the Alte Grenze, where she'd been asked to show up for work at eleven. That didn't suit her at all.

"It's a stroke of luck that you've found work so quickly," he said. "It's only because the cook is unavailable and Helga Seiler has to do the cooking herself. She really needs the help. And you have waitressing experience."

Estelle said nothing. She angrily stared at the road.

"You can't just hang around all day and do nothing. That's no life for a beautiful, inquisitive girl like you."

He felt stupid saying these things, like some old-fashioned pedagogue.

"You sound exactly like my dad, *le salaud*, only worse," Estelle said.

"Well, perhaps your father is right. Alsace is good for people who have their lives behind them. But not for you. You need to be among young people, have stuff going on, stimulation. And if you don't want to learn anything, you have to work. For money, for wages. Doing nothing isn't an option. That's the way of the world."

She gave a derisive sniff.

"Well, what do you want, goddammit?" he shouted.

She looked at him in surprise. "I didn't know you could get angry, *grand-père.*"

"I only want to help you."

"That's what everyone says. But actually they just want to have their way. Because they can't bear it when people lead a different kind of life to theirs. I want to look after Lucie. *C'est tout.* That's what I want."

"But you can't spend your life living with a goat."

"Why not? At least the goat doesn't shout at me."

Hunkeler was about to start shouting again, but he managed to restrain himself. "All right," he said after a while. "We'll keep her. Whenever you come to visit me, you can fetch her from next door and take her for a walk."

"Is that a deal?"

"Yes, it's a deal."

Hunkeler parked on Mittlere Strasse and took the stairs up to his apartment. He went into the kitchen to put the kettle on. Keep calm and drink tea – a useful, comforting adage.

He felt a restlessness inside that he couldn't explain. No doubt the quarrel with Estelle had affected him and perhaps upset him more than he'd realized at the time. It had been a battle really, a power battle. And he had won it.

Hunkeler was sure he had argued and acted correctly. He had defended the old-world values he'd grown up with. Doing nothing wasn't an option.

He drank three cups of tea with a drop of milk, slurping it slowly. He could feel the warmth of the tea spreading across his body, all the way down his arms and into his fingertips. After a while he went into his bedroom and laid down to practise some meditation. He tried for quarter of an hour, but he couldn't get into it.

*Break what's breaking you.* That 1968 slogan had popped into his mind and wouldn't go away. What was breaking him? Or rather, what had broken him? Was he even broken? Had the decades of gruelling CID work ground him down so much that he had turned into a weak-willed underling? Someone who, devoid of all imagination, sung the praise of law and order and regular work? "If you don't want to learn anything, you have to work," he'd said. That statement corresponded with his own upbringing. But was it correct? Hadn't he dreamed of something different? Of living a secluded life in the mountains with a few goats, for example?

No, he didn't feel broken. A bit weary perhaps, a bit worn and battered. But still pretty intact. He hadn't changed the world. But he'd certainly tried to help a little, even if only in a small way.

Nobody had forced Estelle to come to him, he thought. She had come of her own free will. And what she'd got from him was perhaps exactly what she'd expected to get. Advice from the old world. It was up to her to decide what to do with it.

But this wasn't the reason for his disquiet. The real reason was that he hated the thought of going to Waaghof station, where the CID was quartered. It was a new build, all concrete and glass. Everything was dead straight, as if drawn with a ruler. Endless hallways, with numbered rooms so people didn't get them mixed up. Here and there a bit of modern art nobody understood, paid for with public funds. Essentially, it was an enormous machine that evidently functioned very well. It was just that this machine wasn't made for people like Hunkeler.

He'd never felt at home in that building. He'd much rather have stayed in the old Lohnhof. That's why he had put an oak chair in his office. This way the room at least contained one thing that had grown naturally. Apart from Hunkeler himself.

It was like everywhere these days. A few specialists in some administrative department somewhere had access to the tax revenues and used them to build enormous edifices in which people then had to get their bearings. The people themselves weren't consulted.

He remembered a cave in Malta he had visited on a long-ago holiday. The Hypogeum, as the cave was called, had been carved out of the ground several thousand years ago. It was a prehistoric shrine that extended three levels down, the lowest level must have been the most holy. There wasn't a single right angle in that cave, not a single straight line. Everything was round and curved, as if the whole thing had grown organically. And at the very bottom Hunkeler had felt as comfortable as a baby in the womb.

There were several temples on the island from that period, all constructed from the same soft stone that almost looked as if you could eat it. And no right angles, no straight lines here either. They were built in the shape of a clover leaf.

In this culture, there was barely any evidence of men. Only two small reliefs that hung in the museum. They depicted erect penises. Perhaps this was the only aspect of the male that seemed noteworthy to the women of that matriarchal society.

Not a single weapon stemming from that era had been found on the island. What had been found were two large stone statues of enthroned women – corpulent, plump bodies, alarmingly alien to the modern eye. Presumably they were the likenesses of highly esteemed women.

Lying on his bed, Hunkeler realized he'd started to relax and that his breath had slowed. He thought of his mother. An image of her carpet beater popped into his mind. She'd tried to give him a spanking with it once. It hadn't worked, even though he'd held still. They had both burst out laughing.

That carpet beater, like the temples on Malta, had been shaped like a clover leaf. Then he thought of the ruler with which his father had beaten the living daylights out of him.

144

Over nothing at all. Simply to break his will. Luckily he hadn't succeeded.

These were the curious thoughts of Inspector Peter Hunkeler before he dozed off into a restorative lunchtime sleep.

He entered Waaghof station shortly before 3 p.m. Frau Held at reception beamed at him. She was wearing a white blouse, as always, and had applied a touch of rouge. "How nice to see you," she said. "I didn't think you'd be coming back here again. How are you feeling?"

"Like a lonely forest owl that's calling out forlornly into the night. We should get together sometime and share a bottle of wine."

She smiled at him, she seemed genuinely pleased. He was pleased too.

"Still the same smooth-talking charmer. Fear not, I'd certainly hear you calling if you really were. But seriously, Suter is fuming. He's had to interrupt his spring touring week in Arosa. But that's no longer any concern of yours, is it? I bet you're glad."

"I'm not sure. On the whole, I'm happy not to be involved any more. But somehow I'm still an inspector."

"In that case, just come by sometime if you're feeling homesick. Then we'll chat."

"Agreed. I'll do that."

Upstairs in the conference room the entire crew was assembled: Suter, Madörin, Haller and Lüdi. Commissaire Bardet was there too, accompanied by Madame Godet from the Police Nationale in Mulhouse. Kommissar Rotzinger from the Lörrach Landespolizei was also present. That surprised Hunkeler. They only came when the situation was serious.

Brief greetings were exchanged, as always before important meetings. Hunkeler was astonished when Madörin slapped him on the back, presumably with amicable intentions.

Prosecutor Suter, suntanned and sporting a dark blue flannel suit with a gleaming silk tie, welcomed the guests. He wouldn't have called for help across the border if there weren't compelling reasons, he said. The city of Basel – and indeed the entire region, which did, after all, include southern Alsace and Germany's Markgräflerland – were in great danger.

There was a slight quiver in his voice. Suter's talent for the rhetoric of woe was second to none. Madame Godet gave a little cough, Bardet scrunched up his nose in disgust.

"We are here, Madame, Messieurs, to ward off danger and protect our beautiful tri-border area from harm," Suter continued. "Our venerable financial institute, the Basel Volksbank, is subject to grave attacks from unknown parties – attacks that stop at nothing, including murder and manslaughter. As you know, the Volksbank is covered by state guarantee. This means the city of Basel guarantees the savings deposits. If the Volksbank wobbles, then Basel wobbles too. And then the entire tri-border economic hub wobbles, including Alsace and Markgräflerland."

Here Suter paused for effect, to allow the import of his words to hit home.

"*Merde*, why the dirge?" said Bardet. "We in Alsace aren't wobbling."

146

"We in Markgräflerland aren't wobbling either," added Rotzinger.

Suter breathed heavily through the nose several times and adjusted his already impeccably positioned tie knot.

"Please, Madame, Messieurs, bear with me while I give you the facts. The situation is more serious than you may think. About a month ago, Viktor Waldmeier, director of the Volksbank, was arrested in New York upon entering the US. He has now been released following payment of an unknown bail sum, but he's not allowed to leave the country. This would suggest that he's being forced to reveal internal bank data which, according to Swiss law, is covered by banking secrecy. This is a grave attack on our constitutional state. We are determined to oppose this attack with all available means."

"Perhaps the Volksbank should simply disclose its offshore accounts," commented Bardet. "There's French money there too."

"And German money," Rotzinger added.

Suter was visibly struggling to retain his composure. He wasn't used to being interrupted.

"Please, Messieurs," said Madame Godet. "Let Monsieur Suter finish what he has to say."

"Thank you, Madame. Shortly after Waldmeier's arrest, Stephan Fankhauser, long-standing director of the Volksbank and Waldmeier's predecessor, died under somewhat suspicious circumstances. What's clear is that no autopsy was performed, which seems unusual in such a case. I have invited esteemed former inspector Hunkeler to this meeting. He shared a hospital room with Fankhauser. You have all worked with him and I'm sure you remember him well."

At this point Suter attempted a cheery smile, which did nothing to soften the stony expressions.

"Do you have anything to say on this matter, Inspector Hunkeler?"

"No, nothing in particular. I took a sleeping pill that night. I didn't wake up until the morning, by which time Fankhauser was already gone."

"So you were not aware of Fankhauser's passing? You didn't notice anything at all?"

Hunkeler shook his head. He saw that Bardet was grinning at him. "No, nothing at all," he replied.

"In that case, let's turn our attention to the third case," Suter continued after a brief hesitation. "It concerns former councillor Dr Debrunner, who is a member of the Volksbank supervisory board. On his way home from Fankhauser's funeral late at night he was brutally struck on the head, causing him to lose consciousness. He is now recovering, but he can't remember anything. Our forensic department has established that the perpetrator used a fired clay brick for a weapon. Bricks of that nature were found close to Debrunner's house, where some building work is being carried out. Again, there is no trace of the perpetrator."

The wide grin reappeared on Bardet's face. "Someone must have been in a terrible temper," he joked.

"Silence, Monsieur," said Madame Godet.

"I can't bear the atmosphere in this room," Bardet protested. "Who do you take us for? Schoolchildren? What do you want from us, Monsieur Suter?"

"I will come to that in just a minute, Monsieur Bardet," Suter replied, his tone now a shade sharper. "And I would appreciate it greatly if you could bear with me a moment longer. The fourth case concerns Philipp Meierhans, former investment banker at the Volksbank, now retired. He was fatally shot in the Alsatian village of Knoeringue, with his own rifle. He was out hunting at the time. Even though we have offered our help, the perpetrator has still not been tracked down."

Bardet went to say something, but then refrained.

"To summarize," Suter continued, "four important figures connected to the Volksbank have been either arrested or physically attacked. Or have died under uncertain circumstances. We believe that this cannot be a coincidence. Interestingly, all four men were members of a leftist student movement in their youth. The group pushed for revolution. Their aim was to overthrow the entire social order, using force if necessary – they were followers of Marx, Trotsky and Mao. We know that most people involved with the movement have long found their way back into society and pursued a career. But not all of them. The question now is whether these four cases link back to those early years. Could it be that some of those young revolutionaries have since become so radicalized that they want to take revenge on their former colleagues, whom they accuse of defecting to the class enemy? Are we dealing with a kind of settling of scores among former revolutionaries?"

"*Quelle connerie*," Bardet burst out. "Why are you dishing up this bullshit? It's pure nostalgia."

But Suter was not to be dissuaded, he was on a roll. His voice grew sharp like splintered glass.

"What's your view on this, Inspector Hunkeler? You were involved with the 1968 protest movement too."

Hunkeler hesitated before answering. He glanced across at Bardet, whose grin now stretched from ear to ear. "I don't believe the 1968 movement is relevant to these cases," he said.

"I'm not asking you what you believe," Suter replied. "I'm asking you what it was like back then. Tell us about it."

"I was in Prague for a week. I travelled there on a student travel service bus. It was during the time of the Prague Spring. The whole city of Prague was celebrating. It was a celebration of creativity. There was new theatre, new music, new film, new literature on every corner. Back then we believed we could change the world for the better through creativity. We all know how it ended. The Warsaw Pact members sent their tanks and turned Prague into a cemetery."

"I want to know what it was like in Basel," said Suter.

"It was the same in Basel as it was in all university towns. Young people staged an uprising against the Second World War generation. It was the eruption of a volcano that the older generation didn't even know existed. Nobody knew how to respond to this eruption, not even the police. So they let the youngsters carry on. And I would say much was achieved and changed for the better. Of course, it quickly became fashionable to support the Vietcong. And Mao, who was seen as the liberator of the oppressed masses."

"What was the young people's view in terms of violence? Were they violent?"

"Theoretically, many were in favour of so-called revolutionary violence because it was considered necessary to achieve change. Nobody wanted to be a liberal wimp. There was a sort of competition of radicalism. Those who called for violence the loudest enjoyed the highest status. And of course in the safety of our sheltered Basel it was easy enough to do,

150

pushing for revolutionary violence. But in essence, nobody really believed in it. It was the same in Paris that May, when the students occupied the Quartier Latin. I imagine the Parisian police were very surprised at the start of the student uprising when the cobblestones came flying. Students who rip up the paving and throw stones at the police, nobody had expected anything like that. The police could have fired at them, they had the guns. But that would have caused a national uprising. It was this culture, the culture of non-violent conflict, that made the student revolt possible. I think it was no different in Basel."

Suter breathed heavily through the nose several times. This was probably not what he'd wanted to hear.

"I disagree," said Madörin.

"*Mon Dieu*, not that schmuck again," said Bardet. "Do I really have to listen to this?" He got up to leave the room.

"*Non*, Monsieur Bardet," Madame Godet ordered. "Stay and listen."

Bardet sat back down again.

"There was a tendency towards violence from the very beginning of the student revolt," Madörin claimed. "This tendency increased over time. It's true that the majority shied away from violence. But there was a minority that didn't. This minority became radicalized and took action, carrying out terrible attacks on representatives of the system they detested. Look at what happened in Germany and Italy. A part of this minority has persisted to this day. The anarchists. They're highly dangerous. We all know the First World War was triggered by an anarchist, by the Sarajevo assassination. These days, they try to destabilize the system that underpins our society by attacking and paralysing the lifeline it relies on,

151

the banking and financial sector. And the sector is extremely sensitive. We have now arrested a kingpin of the anarchists in Basel and we're holding him on remand. The person in question is a Mr Paul Egloff, who was already advocating for violence against the system back in 1968. He was seen in Knoeringue, close to the crime scene, at the time of Philipp Meierhans' assassination. Of course, this doesn't prove he's the perpetrator, but it's a strong indication. He's still denying it at present, but we'll get it out of him eventually."

An awkward silence spread across the room. Everyone knew Madörin had got completely carried away with one of his madcap theories again. Corporal Lüdi leaned back and closed his eyes. Haller fished his beautifully carved pipe out of his pocket and chewed on it. Even Suter was left speechless.

"Where did you get that information from?" Bardet barked.

Madörin hesitated. He hadn't expected this question, especially not in that tone.

"I heard it."

"I see, you heard it. And I've heard you went to the Knoeringue inn a day after Meierhans' death and asked questions."

"I can drink my coffee where I want," said Madörin. "And I can talk to the landlady if I want to."

But Bardet was only getting started. His voice took on a steely edge.

"I've also heard that you showed up in Huningue a little later, where you monitored Monsieur Egloff's caravan. And without consulting the gendarmerie. What have you got to say to that, Monsieur Madörin?"

Madörin had nothing to say. He looked at Hunkeler for help. But Hunkeler didn't stir.

"This is scandalous, Monsieur Suter. A Basel inspector investigates on his own account in France, without informing us. There are going to be consequences. In the name of the Police Nationale I protest in the strongest terms. The audacity and arrogance of the Basel CID are intolerable. We won't stand for this kind of infringement any more. You're putting our binational cooperation at risk, our cross-border partnership."

Madame Godet remained silent, her eyes downcast. Suter was struggling for words, he didn't know what to say. The attack was too precise, too irrefutable.

Then Bardet's phone rang. "*Je m'excuse,*" he muttered. "I communicated that I was in an important meeting. It must be very urgent."

Bardet took the call. Only his voice interrupted the icy silence in the room.

"*Oui,* Bardet. Really? *Isch das wohr?* And you're sure of that? No, it's OK. I'm on my way."

He ended the call.

"Apologies, Madame, Messieurs, I have to leave the meeting. We have the perpetrator in the Meierhans case. It's a young man from Knoeringue. He and his mother are at the gendarmerie station in St Louis. He says he wanted to take Meierhans' rifle off him because he's against hunting. In the tussle, a shot got discharged. *Bon, c'est tout,* that's it then. Have a pleasant evening."

He got up and walked out.

Nobody said a word. Madörin sat crumpled in his chair. Suter loosened his snow-white collar.

Eventually, Madame Godet spoke up.

"*Bon*, Messieurs, it seems the Meierhans case has been solved. And you can shove your anarchists up your behind. *Bonsoir à tous.*"

Strong words for the prim Madame who usually always strived for conciliation. She marched out stony-faced, followed by Kommissar Rotzinger.

"So there we have it, complete humiliation," said Suter after a while. "What on earth were you thinking, Inspector Madörin?"

Madörin still didn't speak. He looked like a dog who'd been given a hiding.

"You're becoming a bit of a safety risk for this department. Can't you see that? You allow yourself to get too caught up in the thrill of the chase. But Basel is and always will be a liberal city in which dissidents such as anarchists also have their place. We're an apolitical police force. I suggest you get that into your head."

Nervous breathing through the nose. A quick grab of the tie knot – yes, still in the right place.

"I will have to issue a formal reprimand. And please, in future, keep your persecution complex under control. You will immediately release Herr Egloff from custody. This brings the meeting to a close. Goodbye, Messieurs." And with that, he strode out of the room.

Haller put his pipe away and shook his head sadly. Lüdi opened his eyes again and shot Hunkeler a bewildered look. "That somewhat backfired," he commented. "A moderate catastrophe, if I'm not mistaken."

"Well then, my friends," Hunkeler said cheerily, and stood up. "I must be off. It was nice to spend some time with you again." He walked over to Madörin and gave him a slap on the shoulder. "Hard luck, pal. It happens. Just forget about it."

He briefly registered Madörin's hate-filled glance, then he was out the door.

Out on the street he stood still and watched a tram as it rolled past. It was composed of three carriages. It was full, as usual at this time of day. People commuting home to the Swiss suburb of Flüh or the Alsatian village of Leymen. Hunkeler liked that. Let the nations' governments squabble and get into scraps over taxation and freedom of movement treaties. Meanwhile in the Basel region the trams peacefully tootled back and forth over the border.

He strolled over to the Birsig, the little brook that originated in the Leymen valley and flowed straight across the city and into the Rhine. He sat down on a bench under the trees by the embankment. It was a beautiful spring evening, pleasantly warm. The bushes were coming into leaf, the birds were singing. A little further along was the zoo. That was where the storks which were occasionally seen gliding across the sky had their nests.

Hunkeler lit a cigarette, took a deep drag and idly gazed at the embers as they slowly transformed the tobacco into black ash. He took another drag and flicked the butt away in a wide arc.

Everything had worked out well, much better than he'd hoped for. Estelle had found work at the Alte Grenze. Egloff was going to be released from custody. And Moor most likely was back at the Knoeringue inn already.

He resolved to take it easy for a while and spend the next few days in Alsace. Plenty of sleep, leisurely walks, reading. He'd learned enough about the First World War. Hedwig was right, it just made him feel down. He decided to pay the bookshop on Bachlettenstrasse a visit and set off along Birsigstrasse.

The bookshop was the old, traditional kind. A lovely one-man operation that functioned flawlessly. Towers of books everywhere which threatened to come tumbling down but never did. Presumably there was some kind of secret system in the apparent chaos. In any case, the bookseller, a master of literary tower-building, could conjure forth almost any book requested.

"Coming into your shop always gives me a warm glow," Hunkeler told the man. "It reminds me of the old days. It's like an oasis of humanity in here."

"There's not many left of those," replied the man, who looked to be getting on for seventy. "They like to fight dirty these days."

"But not you. You're like a beautiful long-eared owl. You're holding tightly onto your branch."

"A long-eared owl? Aren't they at risk of extinction?"

"How am I supposed to know?"

"Well then, quit the silly analogies. Can I help you, or do you want to browse?"

"I'll have a browse."

Hunkeler found a fat tome on Charlemagne. That sparked his interest. He liked the idea of immersing himself in the world of 1,200 years ago, when medieval Europe was taking shape and the Carolingian minuscule was introduced, the script out of which today's alphabet was developed. Notker

Balbulus popped into his mind, Notker the Stammerer, whose manuscripts were stored at the St Gall monastic library. Was that right? Or had Notker lived earlier? Or later? Once again he realized that, although he'd memorized many names during his university days, he generally had little idea of the people behind those names.

He found a second book that looked interesting, a biography of Otto of Freising. He'd heard about him at university too, without ever finding out why he was an important historical figure. Nobody had explained it to him. And he hadn't had the money to buy books back then. Now he had time and money aplenty, and his thirst for knowledge was just as great.

Around the middle of the week, he finally got to work on that spruce that had toppled over. He chopped off its branches with the large axe. He could feel the blows in his upper arms, it hurt every time the axe struck home. But he kept at it. He started up the chainsaw and brought the saw blade down on the spruce wood. He enjoyed the revving of the engine, the spray of sawdust, the smell of wood and resin. He was going to use the wheelbarrow to transport the lumps of wood to the barn and then chop them into manageable logs. But he would have to leave that for later.

A gendarmerie car had pulled up out on the road. Bardet got out and slowly came sauntering across the lawn. Hunkeler switched off the chainsaw. "Good, come in," he greeted Bardet. "Let's drink a schnapps together."

In the kitchen, Hunkeler poured two glasses of damson schnapps.

"Where is Monsieur Moor?" Bardet asked.

"I imagine he's at the Knoeringue inn. He's a friend of the landlady."

Bardet tipped back his schnapps. Hunkeler topped him up.

"This really is delicious," commented Bardet. "It's just like the one my grandfather used to make. Did you say your neighbour brewed it? Can one buy it?"

Hunkeler got up and fetched another bottle from the bottom of the cupboard. "No. But have this one as a present."

"I can't accept that. You know, bribery and so on."

"Why would I bribe you? Anyway, nobody will know."

"*Bon, merci.* And your granddaughter, Estelle? How is she doing? Is she still sleeping in the barn with the goat?"

"No. The goat is now in the neighbour's cowshed. And Estelle is working as a waitress at the Alte Grenze."

"That's quite a coincidence, *n'est-ce pas?*"

Hunkeler went to refill Bardet's glass, but Bardet declined.

"*Non merci*, not while I'm working. And that's not the only coincidence, is it? First you hide a possible perpetrator. Then you turn up at the caravan site in Huningue, where Monsieur Egloff has his caravan. What's going on here?"

"I drove to Huningue because I wanted to talk to Egloff about Estelle. I only found out about his arrest from the old woman there. I'm sure you've spoken to her."

"And I'm supposed to believe all this?"

"Yes."

Bardet shot him a sharp look. Then he smiled. "*Bon.* If it's the truth, then I'll believe it. It's just unfortunate that I don't know whether it really is the truth."

Now Hunkeler smiled too, all sweet and innocent. "What reason would I have to lie to you?"

158

"That's exactly what I don't know."

Bardet stubbed his cigarette out in the ashtray. "Not that it's any of my business, but what went on with that Dr Fankhauser Suter was talking about?" he asked. "Were you really so fast asleep that you didn't notice anything the night he died?"

"I slept like a log."

"And in the morning, when you woke from your deep slumber, you were alone in the room. *N'est-ce pas?* That was it, was it?"

"Yes, that's exactly how it was."

They both looked out at the garden, where Fritz the cockerel was gearing up to one of his pathetic crows.

"That old cockerel isn't going to last much longer," Bardet commented. "Are you just going to wait for him to drop dead?"

"Why not? What else should I do? Kill him?"

"*Bon.* In that case everything seems to be in order. *Merci* for the schnapps."

The following days, Hunkeler lay on his bed for hours at a time, reading about Charlemagne. About his campaigns against the Lombards in Northern Italy, against the Saxons and the Bavarians, all of which enabled him to expand his empire. About his alliance with the Pope, who in appreciation of all this carnage crowned him emperor and later even canonized him. And here indeed Notker Balbulus appeared. He had been a monk in St Gall and had written an account of Charlemagne's deeds in which he described him as wise and charitable, invincible and incomparable. All of Europe had revered him.

Apart from the Lombards, thought Hunkeler. And the Saxons and the Bavarians.

He read that Harun al-Rashid, the powerful caliph of Baghdad and ruler of the faithful to whom Scheherazade had told the tales of *One Thousand and One Nights*, had wanted to gift an elephant to the great Charlemagne as a sign of his esteem. He sent the diplomat Isaac the Jew on the long journey with an elephant named Abul-Abbas. The odyssey took them by land as far as Tunisia. From there the great animal was transported by boat to Porto Venere in Liguria in the autumn of 801. They overwintered in Vercelli, before crossing the Alps via the Great St Bernard Pass the following spring. And lo and behold, on 20 July Isaac and the elephant Abul-Abbas walked into Aachen.

That amused Hunkeler no end. He laughed out loud when he read about this curious couple that had wandered through countless villages, past astonished onlookers. It was a joyful laughter. He found himself seized with a lust for life and he wondered whether he shouldn't risk a stroll with Madame Lucie after all.

One time, at midnight, the phone rang. It was strange, this ringing in the quiet house in the middle of the night. It spooked Hunkeler. Had something bad happened? Of course not. It was bound to be Lüdi. He shoved the cats off the bed, who mewled in protest, and went out into the hallway to the phone hanging on the wall.

It was Lüdi.

"Did I wake you up?"

"No," said Hunkeler. "I'm reading."

"Oh, what are you reading?"

"I've just read about an elephant that walked all the

way from Baghdad to Aachen with an emissary called Isaac around 800 AD."

He heard Lüdi snigger.

"And why are you reading about that?"

"Because it interests me. Go to the Pfalz terrace above the Rhine sometime and take a look at the Roman chancel of the Minster. You'll see strange animals sitting on the pillars, with enormous trunks, similar to elephants. It's obvious that the stonemasons never saw an actual elephant themselves and only knew about the animal from hearsay. I'm now wondering whether the elephant from Baghdad travelled through Basel. And whether people talked about the strange animal with the trunk for generations. It's an interesting question, don't you think?"

Another short snigger, then the clicking of a lighter.

"We've found the perpetrator in the Debrunner case."

"Have you?"

Hunkeler realized that the Debrunner case no longer interested him in the slightest. And that his feet were getting cold on the tiled floor.

"Aren't you interested?" Lüdi asked.

"I don't know. Not really. Let them bash each other's heads in. What do I care?"

"Well, I'm telling you anyway. It seems the offender is a pensioner who lives next door to Debrunner. He lives alone, but he used to have two Rottweilers. Debrunner made a complaint about them and the pensioner had to give the dogs away. He took revenge on Debrunner by whacking him over the head with a brick. We've found the brick. The pensioner had buried it in his vegetable patch."

"Has he confessed?"

"No, not yet. But it's just a question of time. Anyway, I'll let you get back to your elephant. Sleep well."

Hunkeler stepped outside to relieve himself. He looked up at the sky. An unbelievably vast number of stars twinkled up there.

On Saturday morning, Hunkeler drove to Basel and parked outside his apartment. The air was heavy with the scent of the wisteria and the street was filled with light. Up at the corner, the fountain peacefully burbled away. Its hexagonal trough was carved from limestone and it had three pipes from which the water flowed. Beside it stood benches under a plane tree. It was the only place in this neighbourhood where a traveller could sit down and rest. There were two old women sitting there. They had probably come from the nearby retirement home and were enjoying the warm spring air. Hunkeler greeted them, upon which they interrupted their conversation and eyed him mistrustfully. When they realized it was simply a friendly hello they politely greeted him back.

He strolled on towards Burgfelderplatz. The chestnut tree in the garden of the Sommereck was in flower. He sat down at one of the red tables and looked at the mural that covered the rear wall of the building. It was a depiction of Lake Lucerne and the surrounding mountains. He knew the names of some of them, he had climbed them. When was that? Forty, fifty or sixty years ago? At the bottom right, a rock protruded steeply from the water. It was the Schillerstein, dedicated by the Swiss Confederation to Friedrich Schiller, the author of the *William Tell* play. It reminded him of the

*Rütli-Lied* that he'd crowed along to in school – *von ferne sei herzlich gegrüßet, du stilles Gelände am See. I greet you from afar, oh tranquil land by the lake.*

It took a long time for Edi to appear. He brought Hunkeler a white coffee and the Zurich tabloid. "What are you doing out here?" he asked. "Why didn't you come inside?"

"Because spring has sprung. Haven't you noticed? You should clear up a bit out here and clean the tables. Then you'd have a garden full of customers."

"Heaven forbid," exclaimed Edi. "What would I do with all those people?"

"Serve them food and drink and be a bit friendly, so they enjoy themselves and come back."

"And then it rains for days and I've bought in supplies for nothing. By the way, I've got a nice piece of ham hock in the kitchen, from Wiesental. It's not much, but it's enough for the two of us. How about it?"

"No, not today," replied Hunkeler and took a sip of his coffee.

"What's up with you?"

"Nothing. I'm just in a good mood."

"Aren't you going to read the paper?"

"I haven't read a newspaper all week."

"Well you should." Edi pointed at the tabloid. "It says in there that your colleagues at the CID kept an innocent man locked up on remand for days. It also says that they completely messed up on the Debrunner case. And that the CID is a big pigsty that needs a good clean-out once and for all. What do you say about that?"

"I only read books these days. Have you ever heard of Abul-Abbas?"

"Who's he? Not another one of those terrorists?"

"No," said Hunkeler as he got up. "A peaceful elephant."

He strolled down Missionsstrasse towards the city centre, past the park of the Basel Mission. At the park's centre stood an enormous building surrounded by tall trees. Hunkeler had no idea who worked or lived there. It was a strange concept, he thought, heading out from Basel to evangelize the poor heathens. Who had benefited from this mission? The poor heathens? Or more likely Basel? The old building certainly testified to considerable wealth.

At the Spalentor he turned left towards Petersplatz, where the flea market was in progress. He slowly meandered from stall to stall and looked at the goods on display. He wondered why he'd come here. When he reached the entrance to the university he saw that Mustafa Barikla's van wasn't there. He sat down on the steps in front of the entrance, close to the wall to avoid attracting attention. He sat there for an hour and watched the people as they walked past. Then he got bored.

He went back to the Spalentor and got in the rear carriage of the number 3 tram heading towards the border at Burgfelden. He enjoyed travelling by tram. Rolling along in the middle of the road. The announcement of the stops. The rattling of the wheels as they crossed the intersection on Burgfelderplatz.

On the left stood a shopping centre where you could buy ten different types of bread and twenty flavours of yogurt, all very healthy and guaranteed organic. To the right was the post office. Further along lay Kannenfeld Park, a former cemetery with dark, sad bushes, pools and slides for the kids, benches and a cafe. It was the ideal place for a pensioner, it had everything an old man needed. He resolved to forget about the young woman with the headscarf and cinnamon scent and focus instead on what he saw around him, the sights that this beautiful world presented him with.

He entered the Alte Grenze and sat down at the table by the bar. The place was well frequented. Lunch was macaroni with minced beef and cucumber salad. He also ordered a glass of red wine from Markgräflerland.

Estelle was behind the bar. She was hard at work preparing all the drinks. It wasn't until he grinned at her broadly that she recognized him. She blushed a little, then she decided to smile back.

Hunkeler nodded contentedly. She had evidently managed to stick it out.

He fetched the tabloid paper that was hanging on the wall and read the article Edi had told him about. It was an irate condemnation not only of Basel CID but also the Volksbank and in fact the entire city of Basel. It contained all the typical prejudices, from self-conceit and arrogance through to greed and delusions of grandeur.

It was the same old tune that Zurich so liked to sing. For Basel was a successful city beyond the Jura Mountains, and although it had been part of the Swiss Confederation for five hundred years, it also had close connections to Alsace and Germany's Baden-Württemberg – without asking the rest of Switzerland for permission. And as an urban half-canton it had little regard for the old boorish myths. So for a tabloid keen to up its circulation numbers, there was no harm in having the occasional rant against the unloved city on the Rhine.

All this didn't ruin Hunkeler's appetite in the slightest. He ate the macaroni with relish. In between, he popped a forkful of the lovely, smooth cucumber salad into his mouth, followed by a gulp of Markgräfler wine. A perfect match.

Estelle came over to his table with the coffee.

"How are you?" he asked her. "Come and join me for a minute."

She shook her head. "I need to go and lie down, otherwise I'm going to collapse. It's like a military boot camp in here. Forced labour. On and on, until you fall over. Frau Seiler is very strict. She tells you off."

"Does she? What did she say?"

Now Estelle smiled at him, visibly proud. "She said I can stay. I bet you're surprised, *grand-père*, *n'est-ce pas*?" She planted a kiss on his cheek and disappeared down the hallway.

When the lunchtime rush was over, Paul Egloff came and sat down at Hunkeler's table. He wasn't happy. "What kind of idiots do you have working at your department?" he railed. "I was locked up for days just because I stopped off for coffee in Knoeringue. It's pure tyranny. What country do we live in? The GDR?"

"I'm sorry, but it's nothing to do with me."

"That's what everyone says. Nobody wants to accept blame. But what about my loss of earnings? And compensation? Who's going to pay that?"

"You'll have to contact the department of public prosecution."

"That bloody institution is a complete waste of space. It produces nothing but hot air. Madörin, that blockhead. He isn't just a dimwit, he also suffers from a full-scale persecution complex. Apparently the anarchists are to blame for everything. For the banks going under, the corruption in politics. Probably for foot-and-mouth disease too. Of course, he hasn't got a clue what anarchy means. He thinks he's an upstanding Swiss confederate. But the numbskull can't grasp that our Confederation only operates so well because it has a decentralized, ergo anarchic, structure. All power to the assemblies, that's anarchy, that's Switzerland. Cooperative thinking, cooperative organization. The origins of the Swiss Confederation lie in the old alp corporations of Central Switzerland, which are still going today. Keep as much power in the community as possible. Autonomy in the smallest unit. The interests of Canton and Confederation need to come second. After all, who was William Tell? A freedom fighter, say the politicians in Bern, meaning their own freedom to rule over the population. But that's wrong. Tell was an anarchist."

It was an impassioned tirade that was being poured over Hunkeler. It came from a deeply offended, wounded heart. Hunkeler listened attentively. But his interest evaporated in a flash when he noticed a delicate yet unmistakable scent. A scent of cinnamon.

Instantly, he was on high alert. He tried to keep calm, despite his urge to leap up. He slowly turned his head and saw a young woman with a blue headscarf standing behind his chair. She had her back turned to him and was talking to a young man. She was explaining something to him, gesticulating with both hands. Hunkeler saw that she was wearing a ruby ring on her right middle finger.

He turned back to face Egloff and pretended to be listening to him. Don't go off like a cannonball, he told himself. Don't ruin it again. After a while, he saw the woman walk out with the young man. She hadn't spotted him.

"Who was that?" he asked Egloff. "The woman who left just then. Do you know her?"

"That's Esther Lüscher," Egloff replied. "Why do you ask?"

"I couldn't help notice that she smelled really nice."

"She always smells nice. In fact she's great all round. She's a medical student and she's on the board of the Alte Grenze cooperative. I think she shares an apartment on Rodersdorferstrasse, close to the border. Anyway, you interrupted me. Tell didn't fire that shot for the general public. He was a lone wolf, an inspired character. According to Schiller, Tell said the strong are most powerful on their own. A village community for example is strongest and functions best when it can make its own decisions about village matters. If the villages and towns are disempowered because the power has been transferred to the governing state, then things become dangerous. The rulers of this state inevitably try to wield all the power. If they succeed in doing this – and they almost always do – they come to view the state as their possession with which they can do as they please. The once free farmers then become wage-dependent drudges, free citizens become soldiers and are sent as cannon fodder into murderous wars. And the so-called heads of state don't have to take any responsibility for this whatsoever, even after a defeat that cost millions of lives. At the end of this development stands turbo-capitalism. This integrates the entire world into a unified financial system, which can plunge formerly proud, independent states into ruin with the stroke of a pen. That's why today's big banks are the declared enemies of every self-respecting anarchist. I fight against them by refusing to have anything to do with them. But that doesn't mean I'm going to go and gun down a Volksbank investment banker. There's no point, because behind this investment banker ten more are lurking, eager to take his position. And anyway, I'm against all forms of physical violence. I tried to explain all of this to Madörin, but you might as well be talking to a brick wall."

Hunkeler grinned. "I understand where you're coming from," he said. "I assume your view of things is also the reason why you only provide your productivity and labour to cooperatives."

"Grin away, even I have to laugh at myself. But that's just the way it is. I became an anarchist in my youth because I felt it was the right thing to do. I'm still an anarchist today because I still think it's the right thing to do. I know I'm a spoiled brat. Here in Basel, in the eye of the capitalist typhoon, even an anarchist isn't left to go to the dogs. Even the operation on my cat would probably be paid for by some welfare agency, if indeed I had a cat. It's perverse."

"I think the cooperative concept is compelling," said Hunkeler. "It's clearly working well in this place. Can I join?"

"Of course. Hang on."

Egloff got up and fetched a sheet of paper from behind the bar.

"It's all on here. The statutes, who's on the board. Membership costs two hundred francs per year. You get vouchers, which you can redeem here."

Hunkeler briefly cast his eyes over the paper. Yes, there was Esther Lüscher's name, complete with address and phone number. "Thank you," he said. "So, I'm a cooperative member now."

Hunkeler retraced his steps towards the city centre and turned into Kannenfeld Park. He was walking fast, even though he was in no hurry at all. What should he have done? Leaped up, grabbed the young woman by the arms and confronted her? But what would have been the point? He was no longer a detective, and he had no proof.

He sat down on a bench in the sun. It was surprisingly warm, almost hot even. He looked across at two grandmothers cradling babies in their arms. Judging by their clothing they came from the Balkans or Turkey. As they sat and talked, he noticed they never interrupted each other. One would talk, the other would listen and let her friend finish what she was saying. Only then would the other reply. Every now and then they would gently rock the babies.

Suddenly one of them glanced up, then the other, both looking directly at Hunkeler. They fell silent and sat motionless. He saw fear in their eyes.

Hunkeler could feel sweat beading on his forehead. What the hell was going on? Did they think he was a police officer? A stooge who was out to arrest old women who came from a different country and were perhaps living illegally in Basel?

And they were right, he was a police officer. Or at least he used to be. Was it that obvious? What was different about him compared to other men? He knew from experience that migrants from abroad often had a sixth sense for people in his line of business. Was it never going to end? Once a police officer, always a police officer?

He tried to smile and raised his left hand in greeting. "It's a lovely day, isn't it?" he called across. "Lovely sunshine." He pointed up at the sky.

The women nodded. Then they said something in reply that he didn't understand.

Hunkeler got up and walked towards the exit on wobbly legs.

On Sunday morning he was back in Alsace, preparing breakfast. He put the kettle on, tea for him, coffee for Hedwig. He boiled some eggs, put honey and cheese on the table, bread and yogurt. The kitchen was bathed in sunlight and the two cats were lying on the windowsill, warming their fur.

Shortly after nine the green woodpecker came and landed on the trunk of the half-rotten pear tree in the garden. He appeared every morning, right on time. A green beauty with a bright red head.

The door opened and Hedwig came in, wrapped in her blue dressing gown. Sleepily she padded across to the table, sat down, poured herself some coffee, added a dash of milk and drank. Then she carefully tapped open a soft-boiled egg.

"Are you sure Moor isn't coming back?"

"Yes. The neighbour told me he's back at the Stollers' in Knoeringue. He's going to stay there."

"How do you know that?"

"I have a hunch that he will start painting again soon. What else is he going to do?"

She put some goat's cheese on a slice of bread and took a bite. She did it very slowly, enjoying the humble pleasure of the everyday act.

"And what's your hunch on the young woman with the headscarf and the exquisite perfume?"

"I don't know," he told her. "I'm not quite sure what to do with her."

"Perhaps you should just forget her. What do you reckon?"

"Yes, perhaps. If I can."

"Basically, you need a new job," Hedwig said after a while. "Otherwise you'll keep sticking your nose into things that are none of your business any more."

He shook his head irritably. He didn't like talking about his problems, she knew that. But every now and then she still forced him to.

"A hobby of some kind," she suggested. "Something you find interesting and fulfilling."

He grinned at her, cheekily, even though he knew he couldn't sidestep her. Should he mention the bees, his musings about becoming a beekeeper or a goat farmer?

"I often think about the past," he said. "Especially about my time at university. I was always sniffing around, checking out other subjects. There was this brilliant professor who gave lectures on the Middle Ages. That period still fascinates me. You can get some fantastic books about it now. People know so much. In the old days, a historian only knew about a small part of the period, because the original sources were all scattered across different monastic libraries. Now you can research it all on the internet. Historians can access the information whenever they want and gain a broader understanding."

Hedwig looked at him with surprise while she let honey drip from a teaspoon onto a piece of bread.

"I'm currently reading a book about Otto of Freising," he told her. "Freising is in Bavaria, and Otto was the bishop there. In 1126, when he was fourteen or fifteen, they sent him to Paris to study at the various schools there. With a great big entourage, of course, as he was a member of the high aristocracy. The book describes what Paris looked like at that time. Notre Dame hadn't been built yet. But Saint-Julien-le-Pauvre on the banks of the Seine already existed. And in the nearby abbey of Saint-Germain-des-Prés they had been burying Merovingian kings since the sixth century. That's the part of Paris I was telling you about, where I lived for six months when I was twenty. I often walked to Saint-Julien-le-Pauvre, just because I liked it there. And to Saint-Germain, always shortly before midnight. I didn't know there were kings buried there. It was the illuminated walls that drew me there, the way they shimmered at night. If only I'd had the book about Otto of Freising back then. But of course it hadn't been written yet. When I was in Paris I bought an anthology of Apollinaire's poems. I always had it with me when I was walking around the streets. I would read it whenever I was sitting in a cafe. It was called *Ombre de mon amour*, it was a collection of poems he'd written to his distant lover when he was in the First World War trenches."

She nodded and pushed away her plate. "OK," she said. "Let's go to Paris."

From outside came the sounds of a car door being slammed shut and a vehicle driving off. The front door opened and in walked Estelle, accompanied by a youth with a mop of blonde curls. "This is Jules," she said. "I've brought him with me because he doesn't know where to sleep."

"*Bonjour*," said Jules.

"Well sit down, have something to eat," Hedwig suggested. "I'll make you some fresh coffee."

"*Non, pas de café*," Jules declared. "I need to sleep."

"So who brought you here?" Hunkeler asked.

"Some guy we met in Kleinbasel," Estelle replied. "It's terrible, the boot camp at the Alte Grenze. You're totally worn out before the evening even properly gets going."

"In that case, go and lie down," said Hedwig. "I'll fetch you some pyjamas."

"*Non, pas de pyjama*, I always sleep naked," Jules informed them.

"Right," said Estelle. "We're gonna go and crash. See you later." They heard the two of them go up the stairs.

In the afternoon, Hedwig went to lie in the grass under the plum tree. She needed some peace and quiet, she said, she wanted to read a book on gender studies. When Hunkeler went to have a look, the book had slipped out of her hands and fallen onto the grass. Hedwig was peacefully dozing.

He went upstairs and quietly opened the door to Estelle's room. The two were snuggled up together under the blanket, fast asleep.

Hunkeler went back down to the hallway, picked up the telephone and dialled Lüdi's number.

"Yes, Peter," said Lüdi. "To what do I owe the pleasure on a sacred Sunday afternoon?"

174

"Sorry to disturb you. But there's something that's bothering me."

"No worries. Go on."

"I urgently need some information on someone. Her name is Esther Lüscher. She's a medical student, lives on Rodersdorferstrasse, around twenty-five years of age."

"Esther Lüscher, did you say?"

"Yes. Can you check who she is? Where she comes from? Whether there's anything unusual."

"Happily, but not right now. I'm with my boyfriend, we're sitting outside the Coupole in Montparnasse. That's in Paris, as I'm sure you know."

"Yes, of course," said Hunkeler, who felt rather foolish now.

"Call me tomorrow," said Lüdi. "Around midnight, as always. I'll know more then."

"Thank you, my angel. And say hello to your *joujou* from me."

The following morning he stayed lying in Hedwig's bed for a long time. She got up when her alarm went off and he watched as she put on her clothes with slow morning movements. He heard her clattering about in the kitchen, setting mugs on the table. He listened as she climbed the stairs and gave the young couple a telling-off. It seemed there was some reluctance to get up.

"People who can stay out all night long can also get up on Monday morning," she informed them. "Estelle has to be at work by ten."

A while later he heard the front door close and Hedwig's car drive off. Now the house was silent. All he could hear was the singing of the birds outside – blackbird, blue tit, black redstart, flycatcher.

Nice that I no longer have to rush out, he thought. And: I hope things don't get too complicated with Esther Lüscher.

Around eleven he drove to Basel. He took the route via Knoeringue, he wanted to stop off for coffee at the Stollers'.

Old Moor was sitting at the regulars' table with the land-lady. He had a glass of wine in front of him, but the red haze across his eyes had gone. Hunkeler noticed there was a drawing on white paper pinned up on the wall. A landscape probably, whispered shades of grey delicately applied with pencil.

"Beautiful," commented Hunkeler. "So you're making art again. And from what I can see, with as much skill as ever."

"It's only a drawing," Moor replied. "But it's not a bad way to work. I might buy some paints over the coming days."

"I'm really grateful for what you did," Frau Stoller said to Hunkeler. "He wouldn't have survived being locked up. I'm sure he would have hanged himself."

"Perhaps," said Moor. "Or perhaps not. The need to paint might have kept me going."

"Well, it's all over now," said Hunkeler.


At midnight he rang Lüdi.

"Yes, Peter, you've dragged up a sorry tale there," Lüdi informed him. "Just a sec."

There was a short snigger, then the clicking of a lighter.

"Here it is, I wrote it all down. Esther Lüscher, born 1988, daughter of Anton Lüscher from Sumiswald and Ingrid Lüscher-Weil, born 1958 in Basel. Ingrid's father was called Benjamin Weil. He belonged to a German–Jewish family that fled to Switzerland on 15 February 1939. They came across at Riehen. Two members of that family were turned away at the border. That's all I could find in the records."

Hunkeler was silent.

"Hello? Are you still there?"

"So, a refugee drama," Hunkeler eventually said.

"It seems so. It was a sad time, very sad. And many years ago. Why are you interested?"

Again Hunkeler fell silent.

"As far as I know," Lüdi ventured, "medical students do night duty in hospitals, where they hand out sleeping pills to the poor patients who can't get to sleep."

"Why are you saying that?"

"Just a sneaky feeling I've got. In the meeting a week ago, when you said that you were completely oblivious to everything when Fankhauser died, I didn't believe you. And nobody else in the room believed you either."

Another short snigger, an inhalation of smoke.

"My sixth sense tells me there could be a connection," Lüdi prodded.

"Yes, there could be, but there isn't."

"Be careful what you do," Lüdi warned. "Second World War asylum policy is dangerous territory. But you're old enough."

"Yes, I am. Thank you, my angel."

*

The following morning at nine, Hunkeler phoned Martina Ehringer in Bettingen. It rang fourteen times before she answered.

"I'm the man who ate meat broth with you at the inn two weeks ago," he explained. "I asked you about Stephan Fankhauser. Do you remember?"

"Yes, of course, Monsieur."

"I wonder whether I could talk to you some more about the Second World War. You said you had collected quite a lot of material from that time. I would like to invite you to join me at the inn, if I may."

"I'm afraid that isn't possible, Monsieur. I'm not good on my feet today. Why don't you come to my home, if that suits you. At three o'clock, for tea."

"That would be lovely," said Hunkeler.

Frau Ehringer lived in a small farmhouse not far from the inn. She led him into the front room. The table was neatly laid, with a white linen tablecloth and a fine porcelain set decorated with little roses. She herself was wearing a lily-white blouse. She poured the tea and waited until he had stirred in some sugar and taken the first sip. It was finest-quality Chinese smoked tea.

She pointed at a wall covered with photocopied sheets, all neatly secured with pins. "Here's my museum," she said. "This is my parental home, a kind of mausoleum. The bits of paper on the wall are all stories that I have kept because somebody should know about them. Otherwise they'll be forgotten."

She stood up, hobbled over and tapped on individual sheets with her walking stick.

"Each sheet tells the story of someone's fate. Of Jews who tried to flee to Switzerland. From 1938, they had to have a

178

large red *J* entered into their passports. And the Swiss border guards had been instructed to send Jews straight back. The government in Bern had decreed that. Without informing the population, however.

"And there were other people too who got turned away. Polish forced labourers for example, from the Wiesental region. They weren't let in either. Not long before the war ended, three Poles were shot by the Gestapo just across the border in Lörrach. It was only in the very final days of the war that the border was opened for them. At that time, around fifteen hundred forced labourers came across into Switzerland via Riehen within the space of a few days."

She was talking like a teacher in a history lesson. She was well prepared.

"The sheet up there tells the story of a man who only just made it to the Bettingen customs house. There he asked to be given the last rites. When he'd received them from the clergyman who'd been called, he died. Later they found out that he was a German priest."

"Where did you get all these reports from?"

"I have a whole lot more of them," Frau Ehringer said, and opened a large cupboard. It contained stacks of paper, carefully ordered and filed. "Of course, I was too young at the time to fully understand what was happening. But as I never married, I've had plenty of time to ask people what it was like. I also talked to people across the border, in Lörrach and Inzlingen. And I went to the customs offices, where I read through the chronicles and made copies of anything interesting." She sat down and looked at him expectantly.

"Goodness, you've put together a whole archive."

She smiled proudly. "Yes. It's just a pity barely anyone wants to know about it. You're one of a very few. Would you like some more tea?"

"Yes please."

As she poured, she held onto the lid of the pot to stop it from falling. Her hands were completely steady.

"I'm interested in a family by the name of Weil," he told her. "They came across the border at Riehen on 15 February 1939."

"That's not quite correct. I remember that case well. The Weil-Klein family consisted of five people. The young couple with their little boy, Benjamin, and two elderly sisters. The couple and Benjamin managed to get across the border. The two old women didn't succeed. They tried it first. They ran into the hands of border guards, who took them to the customs building. There they were registered and then sent back."

She got up, searched around in the cupboard for a while, took out a sheet of paper and laid it on the table.

"This is the border control log for 15 February 1939. It states that two old women were apprehended in the Eiserne Hand area. The Eiserne Hand is a stretch of land that juts out a long way into German territory. Many refugees tried to get across there. The border guards knew that and kept a lookout. The two sisters were called Debora Weil-Klein and Mirjam Klein. They were well over seventy."

"Was anything ever heard from them again?"

"Not as far as I know. Anyone who was sent back inevitably ended up in the clutches of the Gestapo. The three others, the couple and little Benjamin, then managed to get across undetected because the border guards were busy with the two women."

"So they sacrificed themselves to clear the way for the others," said Hunkeler.

"It's possible, yes. I don't have any written information about the young Weil-Klein couple. Everything I know about them, I got from talking to old Frau Weber, the baker's wife. She passed away many years ago, and the bakery doesn't exist any more.

"The young family managed to reach the village. They took their chances and entered the bakery. They were exhausted and frozen through, Frau Weber told me. She took them into the back of the bakehouse to warm them up and give them something to eat. And probably also to hide them. If they had fallen into the hands of the border guards, they would have most likely been sent back too. The border guards were under the command of the federal government, not the cantonal authorities.

"At that time, a man called Heinrich Rothmund was chief of the Swiss immigration office. With the backing of the responsible federal councillor Johannes Baumann, he had issued the directive that all Jewish refugees should be prevented from entering the country. These were the people who pulled the levers, who fought against the '*influx of foreigners and particularly Jews into Switzerland*,' as Rothmund wrote. They were in Bern, far away from it all. They didn't see the refugees. They just wanted them gone. Out of sight, out of mind. Although for the sake of historical accuracy I should add that the big extermination camps in the East hadn't been built yet at that time.

"The regional administration in Basel didn't agree with the government's inhumane, racist asylum policy. Fritz Brechbühl, a Social Democrat, was chief of the Basel police back then. He'd been sent out to work from a young age and had experienced plenty of hardship and misery himself. With the support of the predominantly left-wing governing council he issued an order that any refugees who were picked up by the police could only be sent back with his consent. People in Riehen knew that. And Frau Weber knew it too. She arranged for the young couple and little Benjamin to be taken to the Lohnhof station. That's how they were able to stay."

"It makes me want to puke," Hunkeler blurted out. "Please excuse my language. But all of that business, it's unbearable."

"I disagree," Frau Ehringer said with a kindly smile. "Not all of it is sickening. We can also be a little bit proud of Basel. The city largely stood up to the pressure from Bern. We in Basel personally witnessed the refugee misery. It's easy to turn away a refugee when you're sat in an office in Bern. It's not so easy any more when you have the refugee right in front of you."

She smiled at him again. She was enjoying having an audience.

"The fight against the directives from Bern continued. On several occasions, the quarrel turned ugly. The government insisted on its legal authority to issue directives. The federal immigration office didn't want to tolerate that Basel was making its own decisions on immigration matters. At one point, when a group of Jewish refugees came across, they demanded that at least '*six of the younger individuals without dependants*', as they put it, should be sent back. Again, Fritz Brechbühl didn't pay them any heed. Here, I'll show you something. Read this."

She hobbled back over to the cupboard and fetched a piece of paper.

"This here is a report from the Basel immigration police to their departmental director. It's dated 15 March 1939."

Hunkeler read the report.

*In line with our sympathetic approach to immigration issues since the commencement of emigration from Germany, we have not implemented the deportations to German territory requested by the federal immigration office. We were first and foremost guided by humane considerations. Anyone who is directly involved with the immigration problem cannot fail to see that the deportation of these 140 people is not reasonably possible. And in any case, the citizens of Basel would sharply condemn its immigration authority for any such action, as it contradicts the city of Basel's tradition of charity. Our humane approach was, at all events, in line with the intentions of our departmental director and the governing council.*

"I have lived in Basel for several decades now," Hunkeler reflected. "I like living here. And after reading this report I like living here even more."

He lifted the cup to his lips and slurped down the rest of his tea. The cup sat light as a feather in his hand.

"Why is this text not known about?" he asked Frau Ehringer.

"Because people don't like to talk about that part of our history. People want to forget."

Hunkeler put the cup down and gathered his thoughts.

"What was the name of the border guard who signed the log for 15 February 1939? I can't read this old handwriting."

"It was Steffi's father, Joseph Fankhauser."

"Has anyone else apart from me shown any interest in this information recently?"

She nodded. "Yes. It was about a year ago. A history student contacted me because she wanted to write a paper on the refugees that arrived in Riehen. She said she would send me her text, but I never received anything from her."

"Can you remember her name?"

"Yes, of course, Monsieur. Her name was Esther Lüscher."

"In that case I must thank you very much. You have helped me a lot."

"My pleasure."

Leaning on her stick, Frau Ehringer led him to the door.


On his way home, Hunkeler parked by the St Johann river lido on the left bank of the Rhine. The lido was already in the shade, but out on the water the late afternoon sun still shimmered and the opposite bank was bathed in sunlight.

The river was running high with meltwater, as always in spring, and the water was a refreshing thirteen degrees. He slipped into his swimming trunks regardless and dived head-long into the flow, which enveloped him like a cloak of ice. He let himself drift for a while, without breathing. Let's see who's stronger, he thought, the cold fingers of death or my warm heart. He could hear faint sounds from the riverbed, where the pebbles were being pushed towards the sea. A delicate, silvery rippling.

He got back out by the second set of steps, shook the water from his body and dried himself off. Even for that short space of time, it had felt good being one with the river, the flow that connected the snow in the mountains with the salt water of the ocean.

He bought a hot coffee at the kiosk and sat down at one of the little tables. He listened to the rumbling of the Rhine that he had just climbed out of.

Back at home, he dialled the number for Esther Lüscher. He got the answering machine.

"Frau Lüscher, please listen," Hunkeler said onto the tape. "I'm the old inspector who shared the room with Stephan Fankhauser when he died. I'm retired, I no longer have any official authority. In any case, Stephan Fankhauser has long been laid to rest. I don't want anything from you, I just want to talk. I know two things. Firstly, that Debora Weil-Klein, who I assume was your great-great-grandmother, and her sister Mirjam Klein were sent back across the German border at Riehen in February 1939. And I know that the border guard responsible was Joseph Fankhauser, Stephan Fankhauser's father."

Here he paused. He took a breath, then he continued.

"I'm begging you, talk to me. Otherwise I'll never get any peace of mind."

The phone was picked up. A woman with a young bright voice asked: "What do you want from me?"

"I want to talk to you."

"OK then, you stubborn idiot. Meet me at the Linde, Au Tilleul in French, in an hour. It's a couple of hundred yards beyond the border at Burgfelden." She put down the phone.

Hunkeler set off, on foot. He wandered along the Burgfelderstrasse towards Alsace. Past Kannenfeld Park, past the Alte Grenze. To his right stood the newly built retirement complex, with apartments for old people who could still walk in a straight line and tip a can of peas into a pan. A sort of hellish anteroom to the hell of the nursing home, he thought and quickened his steps. As yet he was nimble on his feet and determined to escape the Grim Reaper.

On the left was the turn-off for Theodor Herzl-Strasse, which led to the Israelite cemetery. He came to the border crossing, which could only be accessed by vehicle from the French side. As usual, there was nobody on duty. The final stretch of the road was lined with single-storey Alsatian houses, illuminated by the evening sun.

The garden at the Linde inn was open, which was rare. The Alsatians preferred to sit inside. He ordered a coffee and waited, feeling profoundly insecure and as nervous as a schoolboy outside the headmaster's office.

Esther came cycling along on a red bike. She wasn't wearing a headscarf and he noticed her beautiful black hair. She sat down with a grim, angry expression. He could smell her perfume, the hint of cinnamon.

"So, what do you want?"

"Wouldn't you like something to drink first?" he asked.

"No. What is it you want to say."

"I told you on the answering machine the things I already know. I assume that the quick, painless death was a release for Stephan Fankhauser. Nevertheless, as far as I'm informed active euthanasia isn't permitted in hospitals. And that was more than active euthanasia. Fankhauser tried to fend you off."

"Do you seriously think I've got any idea what you're talking about?"

"Yes, I think you do."

She made a move to get up, then hesitated. She decided to stay.

"That week, Lydia Siegenthaler was on night duty," he said. "Like you, she always wore a headscarf. She's the same build as you, but her eyes are different. She wears a different ring. And she doesn't smell of cinnamon. That's why I realized it wasn't her."

She fixed him with her greenish-grey eyes. He'd seen that cold gaze before. "I stepped in for Lydia Siegenthaler that night because she wanted to go to a birthday party," she said. "We didn't notify anyone because they always make such a fuss at the Merian Iselin Hospital when you change anything. Nobody noticed. Apart from you. It isn't a crime to stand in for a colleague."

"But it's a crime to inject a dying person with a lethal substance against their will."

She smiled at him sweetly. "Are you saying somebody did that?"

"Yes, I'm sure of it."

"Then why didn't you report it?"

"The following morning I spoke to the doctor. I asked him who had been on duty the previous night. He said it was Lydia Siegenthaler, and that everything had run its proper course. I had nothing concrete, no proof. Just a recollection of something before I sunk into a deep sleep. A hallucination perhaps. I felt bewildered. But now I know that it wasn't a hallucination."

"Oh, that's what you meant by peace of mind. Enjoy the rest of your evening." She went to get up.

"Wait," he said. "I haven't finished yet." He searched his pockets for a cigarette, found one and lit it.

"Nervous, are you?" she asked.

"Of course. What do you think? I feel ashamed of the Swiss government's asylum policy in the Second World War. It is and always will be a disgrace for Switzerland. It's not an easy thing to come to terms with, even for someone born after the event."

"Goodness, spare me the tears. This is ridiculous." She swept her hair aside with her hand. She was furious now.

"Where did you get the ruby ring you're wearing?" he asked.

"From the woman who was my great-great-grandmother. Before she set off across the border, to supposed safety, she gave this ring to her son with the instruction to pass it onto his eldest daughter. As he never had a daughter, he passed it onto his son Benjamin, who gave it to his daughter Ingrid Lüscher-Weil. I am Ingrid's eldest daughter. And I'll tell you one more thing. I don't believe in Christian charity. What that charity amounts to was clear to see in the Second World War. They were all Christians, those people who rampaged and murdered. And when someone sends two old women back to certain death, they don't deserve forgiveness."

"But it wasn't Stephan Fankhauser who sent them back. It was his father."

"God's vengeance, as you may know, carries on to the third and fourth generation."

Hunkeler shuddered at the sound of those words. He shook his head, very slowly, several times. Then he asked: "What were you doing up in the gallery of the Minster after Stephan Fankhauser's funeral?"

She went pale and it took her a second to regain her composure. Her pride won over.

"I blessed the Minster because the city of Basel took in my great-grandparents and my grandfather in 1939. If it hadn't, I wouldn't be sitting here at this table with you now. Right, that's it. And don't bother me again."

She got up, jumped on her bike and cycled off.

Hunkeler was sitting on the train to Paris with Hedwig. He had insisted on taking the ordinary direct train, not the TGV. He said he wanted to enjoy the journey. He wanted to gaze out of the window and watch the countryside glide past. The ruins of the old fortifications at Belfort. The chapel of Ronchamp, which could only be glimpsed briefly between the forested hills. The vast plain of Vesoul, the dark walls of Troyes. Then the arrival, rolling into the north of Paris, with the domes of Sacré-Coeur high up to the right. That wasn't possible in the superfast TGV, it made you go all dizzy when you looked outside, he'd said.

They were sitting in the restaurant car, eating croque-monsieurs and drinking coffee. Up to the left, on an outstretched hilltop, Langres Cathedral glowed white in the afternoon sun.

Hedwig sat there like a purring cat. "We should do this more often," she said. "We'll go and visit the Musée de Cluny and look at the Basel altar frontal. We'll go to Saint-Julien-le-Pauvre and light a candle. And we'll sleep wonderfully at the Louisiane."

Hunkeler nodded. Yes, that was what they were going to do.

"So, what about your cinnamon-scented woman?" she asked. "Did you find out anything more?"

"The matter has resolved itself. It must have been a hallucination."

Hedwig shot him a suspicious glance, she didn't believe him.

"No really, it's all done and dusted," he assured her.

He lifted the music box out of the bag, wound it up and placed it on the table. Then he let it run. A musette waltz, light and delicate, rose from the box. He quietly hummed along to it.